ROSS HALL

ROSS HALL

ANDREW KEY

grand IOTA

Published by
grand**IOTA**

2 Shoreline, St Margaret's Rd, St Leonards TN37 6FB
&
37 Downsway, North Woodingdean, Brighton BN2 6BD

www.grandiota.co.uk

First edition 2021

Cover and title page images: two details from the portrait (1781)
by Joseph Wright of Derby of Brooke Boothby reading
Rousseau's *The Confessions*
Author photo by Laura Gill

Typesetting & book design by Reality Street

A catalogue record for this book is available from the British Library

ISBN: 978-1-874400-84-4

During Jean-Jacques Rousseau's stay at Wootton Hall in Staffordshire, where he spent a little over a year between 1766 and 1767, the local population, unaccustomed to French surnames and how to pronounce them, called him "Ross Hall". In June 1840 the writer William Howitt travelled to Wootton in search of any traces of Rousseau's sojourn there. In his book, published later that year, Howitt recounts meeting various residents of Wootton who had heard of Rousseau, as well as a few elderly men and women who, as children, had seen him with their own eyes. He records meeting James Robinson, "a blithe old fellow of about ninety": "When I asked if he knew the Frenchman who once lived at Wootton Hall, he replied, 'What, owd Ross Hall? Ay, know him I did, well enough. Ah've seen him monny an' monny a time, every dee welly, coming and going in's comical cap an' ploddy gown, a'gethering his yarbs.'" Rousseau cut a strange and exotic figure in this remote region, but was still remembered decades later as being very kind to the poor.

Snow, still. Standing outside the coach, salt-grey clouds low above, stopped by a fallow field, a howling and bitter wind, a few flecks whirling around me, my robe hitched to my waist, desperate, desperate, straining to relieve some of the ruinous pressure in my bladder, my teeth chattering, mucus beginning to stream from my eyes and nose, ears and skull aching as if in a vice, straining, willing with all the energy I can muster, urging more than just a few drops of urine to spill on the ground. The briefest trickle stains the grey snow dark brown, almost red. A moment of relief; a shooting pain through my kidneys, but no worse than the desperation before. No worse, just different. I drop my robe, my legs numb from the cold. I rush back to the coach. I feel better. I sit. I exhale and rub my hands together to warm them. I pull the squirrel-fur cap down over my ears. I think I see Thérèse smile across at me, but it's dark, even though it must only be midmorning. She says nothing. Sultan rests his head on my lap, his breath forming small clouds. The relief lightens my spirits and I start to hum the melody I've been working on since Môtiers. The coachman shouts and the wheels turn. On. I feel hopeful, for a moment. And then, as soon as this scant minute of hope apportioned to me is over, the old pressure returns, the ache, the restlessness, the need to disburden myself. My urethra stings. My lower back feels as if it had a knife in it. I squeeze my legs together and close my eyes. This ailment has been with me my entire life and it always reduces me to feeling like an infant, a young boy, needing to piss but not being allowed, the sad pathetic desperation of holding yourself together, the humiliation of incontinence. How often I've felt my cheeks blaze from the shame. I can't ask to stop the coach again, not so soon. It is difficult making myself understood to the driver, who doesn't share my language. Further humiliations. I couldn't relieve myself in the coach even if I wanted to. The strain required to squeeze little more than a teaspoon out of myself is too much to repeat more than once every twenty minutes, though the urge is there. I am exhausted. The returning pressure makes me want to weep. I want my mother, who I never knew, and I want Maman, who served as my mother when I was a lost adolescent, my first lover, my true friend. Sultan dozes on my thigh and breathes a deep sigh. I squeeze my eyes shut, clamp my legs tight. I rock back and forth a little, trying to breathe deeply and to calm myself. The wheels of the coach churn in the mud outside, the snowfall gets heavier, I can feel every passage and tube in my body taut in the icy cold. I am in England. I am going to be alone, finally. Finally, alone.

The wheels churn in the mud and the coach rolls forward. It snows. The snows started in October and haven't stopped since, no matter where we go. Now it is March, and I am further north than I have ever been before. When it doesn't snow, it rains; a constant stream of moisture, never heavy, usually just drizzle, soft, just as the snow is never particularly heavy here. There is a constant dampness in the air. We have been travelling for a few days now, stopping as infrequently as possible; I am eager to reach the house as soon as we are able. The horses have to rest, of course, and so does the driver, but I am forced to be attentive when we do stop, to make sure neither the driver nor Thérèse drinks too much at the inns. At our last stop – I don't know the name of the village, the inn had a sign painted with a fox and three ducks – I went upstairs to try to steal some sleep in a bed for a few hours and came downstairs to find our driver slouched drunk and snoring in front of the fire, an empty vessel broken at his feet, with Thérèse in stilted but flirtatious conversation with a man who appeared to have no teeth in his skull. We must move on. The feelings I have about the journey are ameliorated by the great relief I feel at leaving London: too much activity surrounded me in the city; I found myself overwhelmed, incapable of snatching any time to myself, away from the hordes of people attracted by my name. Of course this is flattering, but I am suspicious and leery of too much attention. Hume has done a lot, both to protect me from the mob and to introduce me to the worthwhile people in the city, but I feel most grateful to him for his arranging my stay in the country, away from all the people with designs on my time, out of the clamour and filth of London which, like Paris, resembles nothing more than it does an open sewer. Yes, David has shown himself to be a true friend already; he has expended a lot of time and energy to help me – after all, I was a stranger to him only a few months ago. He can't hope for much reward from his good actions, but I can repay him to some degree with my respect and my love, and by showing him the high regard in which I keep him in my heart. He is a good man, surely one of the best in Europe. If the house he has arranged for me lives up to its promise, then I'm quite sure that I will be happy there for many years to come. This country feels unpeopled: it seems like for days now I have seen nobody outside the coach window, just endless dark-brown fields with patches of dirty snow, some crows. Occasionally we might pass a man, ragged and bent, perhaps with a load on his back, slowly making his way in the same direction as us, surrounded on all sides by grey, black, brown shades, shivering in the snow, an apparently unending trudge onwards, back to some hole. These sights depress me greatly; so different from the images of the rustic and joyful country life which I retain from the other places I have lived, particularly from my childhood. The peasants of the Vaud, for instance, strong, hearty, open in their hearts and expansive in their generosity, framed by deep, lush greens and bright blue skies. Naturally I exaggerate, the Vaud is dismal in winter, like anywhere else; it is too easy to let nostalgia and fondness for those people carry me away, now that I have been forced to seek asylum overseas, jettisoned and expelled out of my homeland, which I can never hope to see again, or enjoy as a free man, the citizen I once was. I might only return again as a corpse, if ever I do at all.

It was still cold when we reached the house, isolated, not very large – smaller than I had expected – but well-maintained. The trip had increasingly taken us through valleys and over hills, through darkening landscapes. Endless drystone walls divide the fields. In London they had told me that the countryside was not unlike that surrounding Geneva. I wasn't quite convinced. But it seemed nice enough, other than the cold and the rain. Pleasant, gentle. The house is halfway up a valley. Various even promenades have been built, surrounding the accommodation, ranging up and down the slope, with some really wonderful lawns, some of the finest, most beautiful lawns I have ever seen – even in the unflattering and dull light of a late winter's day. The view from the front lawn of the house extends for some miles. More fields, divided by stone walls, scattered farms, some slightly more ornate houses dotted here and there, I imagine inhabited by bluff and cheerful country squires. My host has not told me much about my neighbours. Some copses, some larger woods. The horizon is ringed by gloomy and lofty slopes; dark brown, nearly black towards the summits. I am told that in summer they will be purple with heather, but now they look as though nothing could live on them. The surrounding landscape is full of rabbits, apparently, and some pasture, mostly sheep. There is a heavy sense of sparseness here. The wind howls down the valley, rattling the windows of the house. Bitter. Allegedly it will be calmer in summer. Yes, it seems fine here. I feel some hope. We were greeted at the house by a few servants. I have no idea how we will communicate, since Thérèse and I do not speak English, and the local dialect is so murky and opaque that even if I were fluent I should think I would never be able to understand them here. They, of course, know no French. But we smiled at each other readily, and they greeted us kindly, with real warmth, as though they were pleased to have guests on whom to tend. Thérèse was also pleased. The only stain on our arrival was the lingering matter of the carriage. Davenport and Hume had both insisted that it would be returning here anyway, and so the matter of payment was irrelevant. Of course, I saw this as a deception. There is a kind of politeness and generosity at work in my host which I cannot stand; I have to refuse it. I have agreed to pay Davenport for the use of the house. I pay him rent, I am his tenant. I have also refused to receive my letters here, because of the costs, and Davenport has agreed to bring them when he visits in a few months. Good. He knows my financial situation, but he knows too that I pride myself on my independence. I must insist to him again that I pay for our transportation. What seem to be the kindest gestures are always snares with which they hope to entrap you. Friendships based on gifts cannot be true friendships. They become sour. Business transactions. Give me nothing and I'll give you nothing in return – nothing other than myself, as open and as honestly as I can render myself. A gift, especially one of money, is an obligation I cannot repay, and one I must refuse to accept. I refuse to be indebted to any one. I refuse, I refuse. I must strive to maintain my own independent position. Davenport must be made to understand this. I don't suppose that he intends any thing sinister behind his kindnesses; neither he nor David mean to make me feel trapped. I suppose I am too sensitive. As I alighted from the post-chaise I tried to press some money into the driver's hands. After all, despite his drinking, he had kindly stopped so many times because of my indisposition, and it had been a long and uncomfortable journey. He looked pained and tried to give me back some coins. Clearly he had his instructions. One of the servants stepped forward, they exchanged some words off to one side. Thérèse looked irritated. I immediately felt again as if I were a small child; one who had committed some offence, the nature of which I did not understand. After some further discussion between them, the driver came to me, hat in hand, and gave me the money back. He said something I didn't catch, bowed slightly and returned to the vehicle, where he busied himself with the horses. I looked to the servant for an explanation, but he merely smiled, and began to usher me indoors. I looked back at the driver, but it was too late. I must write to Davenport immediately.

The snow will not melt. I try to walk out in the country, but the lanes are impassable, the wind is too cold, and after hardly any time at all I am forced to turn back, exhausted from tramping through the mulch and the deep banks of snow. The house is dark and silent, the ticking of a clock, some panes of glass rattling or cracking, branches tapping against windows, floorboards creaking, a slight murmur coming from the servants' quarters or the kitchen, Sultan yawning and padding about the room, logs crackling. All day long the sky is dark; we have to have candles even at midday; everyone is wrapped up in many layers, it is cold, biting. The earth seems to be dead though the first flowers should be blooming. Apparently I am too late for the snowdrops and the crocuses – there should be daffodils and bluebells by now, but of course I can't get out to see them. The trees are skeletal. It is as if I am in some cold antechamber, waiting for something to happen, for an appointment that has been delayed. All that I can do is remain where I am, hoping that sooner

or later I will be summoned to wherever it is I am supposed to be going, to whatever appointment I have
been waiting for, and that I will be seen by the judge
that has summoned me. After the panic and activity of
the journey here, my flight from Switzerland, my time
in Paris, in London, I was at first glad for the opportunity of some peaceful idleness, but this staying inter-
minably inside is beginning to feel like imprisonment;
I feel that I am being held in abeyance, that a judgment is about to fall on me from some unknown and
unknowable authority, that I must remain still, with
no news from the outside world, while those who wish
me ill, the Inquisition out there, are free to manoeuvre
and to scheme, to advance their plot against me. I am
out of the world and they are in it, and I can garner no
advantage from my isolation if I cannot manage to distract myself, if I am held hostage by the terrors of my
own imagination and the febrile business of an inact-
ive mind – flickering between wild illusion and the
boredom of total stasis. I sometimes sit at the spinet,
but the notes I play seem to disturb the dark stillness
of the house too violently, and feel as if I am imposing
on the gloom.

Some of the neighbours have heard of our arrival. Despite the lingering snow and the harsh wind, they have
made their way over to the house. At first I welcomed
them when they came, hoping for friendly distractions
– if not for me, then at least for Thérèse – but I was
quickly disappointed. They are typical representatives

of the grasping middle classes, tenant farmers who have made enough money to no longer have to dirty their own hands with harvesting the crops or tending to the sheep. Middlemen, only interested in accumulation. They gawp at my attire, they snub Thérèse – most of them can barely communicate with us, speaking our language haltingly and with many errors. I might perhaps be capable of understanding them better if I had a reason to make the effort; but luckily I can use the fact that I have almost zero knowledge of their language as a barrier, as an excuse to keep them away from me. I have stopped admitting them. I doubt that Davenport will mind, since I believe he is of the genuine aristocracy of the country, or is rich enough to be, and would have no dealings with them himself – of that I'm certain. I would gladly make friends with the genuine working people of the area, if only we could talk to each other. I'm sure that if we shared a language we would like exactly the same things. I have simple tastes. On an attempt at an excursion the other day, I watched the workers leaving the nearby lead mines, just a short distance from the house. They were walking home after work, breath freezing in front of them in the cold air, and I longed to speak to them, to offer to share a ready and easy meal of bread, cheese and beer with them perhaps, but I was too shy. Perhaps soon I will be brave enough to talk to them, emboldened by the lack of other company. But finally I have the solitude I have yearned for, which I have needed for so long, and so I will keep to myself and my own company for the foreseeable future. That class of improving mediocrities who think they have elevated themselves, who seek to domesticate nature only to wrench some extra profit from her – those people can mean nothing to me. And likewise: what can I be to them, other than some freakish entertainment sent to amuse them; some foreign eccentric, some exiled lunatic.

I am settling in. A routine has started to establish itself. Since I receive no correspondence here I feel in fact quite free. Davenport will come at the end of next month, six or seven weeks perhaps, and until then no letters. Here I am left to myself. Though the house receives a few of the newspapers from London, which Mr Walton, Davenport's agent – who administers the estate here – leaves around for me to look at. My name appears more frequently than I would have expected, though not always in a kindly light. When I first arrived here the papers were full of acclaim for me and my name. What accounts for this change? Outside, the weather is still bad: bitter winds which cut the face. Every room in the house feels damp. But I don't mind too much. Thérèse likes our situation less than I do. She throws open the windows to try to air out the rooms, and is forced to close them again immediately when the wind comes in. Often it rains. The variety of rains feels unlimited, but really it just oscillates between two modes: heavy downpours that lighten to a misty drizzle, into which one is absorbed fully, before the intensity picks up again and the drops fall like lead. The snow is gone now, at last, and some-times I can go out further into the hills. Not as often as I would like, but sometimes. I am pleased with the countryside around here now that I have started to get to know it. The lichens and mosses are especially delightful. The restriction of my mental horizon to the microcosmic beauties of plant life is one of the few consolations left to me on this earth, and I hope to spend my last years focused on my botanical studies, which never seem to progress, which move about in circles of forgetting and remembering, rotating on the same spot, without utility or value to any one else, but which for that reason are all the more precious to me. If I follow the banks of the stream as it winds away from the house there are various nooks in which one finds the most wonderful specimens. Yes – this is all I want from life now, to be out of the world and free to roam about among the plants. I would rather live in one of the rabbit warrens in the countryside here than in the most luxurious apartment in London. It is important that while I am here I continue to work on the manuscript of my memoirs. I have given up on all other projects now, after my last abandoned attempts to develop a system of legislation for the Corsicans. I no longer want to be seen as a writer or a philosopher in the eyes of the world, and maybe if I complete my recollections of the life I have led I will at last be able to quench this compulsion to write things down, and finally be granted by God the quietness of mind that I will need to enjoy my last years on this earth. I had thought briefly of writing a compendium of plants, a botanical encyclopaedia, but the task is too great for me to complete, my knowledge is inadequate. But I hope while I'm here to be able to expand that small knowledge somewhat, to collect specimens of the local flora. If I can divide my time between revisiting the happy hours of my youth and walking the hills and collecting plants, then I'm sure I will be quite content here, even in spite of the weather. The foreignness of the language, the removal from the world, those elements of this situation which would be offputting to others, are what suit me best about this place. Yes, I think that I might indeed be quite comfortable and satisfied here, and I must write again to David to thank him for his efforts in finding such a suitable residence for my wants.

The boundaries marked by the stone walls are relatively recent, I am told. Yes, Mr Walton and I have our small conversations: he speaks passable French, but can't get too far into any thing. And our distance in social position, he being employed by my host, keeps us from any real intimacy. I asked him about the walls, some of which are unfinished, large piles of small rocks standing abandoned out in the country. A new series of gridlines cut through the landscape, curving off gently into the horizon. The sheep here, instead of roaming where they want accompanied by some barefoot shepherd, are lodged within one stone boundary until they have cleared the ground of every morsel, then they are moved to the next section within the network of walls to repeat the experience. This land is all owned by someone or other now, the old customs of commoning understood as inefficient ways of tending to it, much more can be wrenched from nature this way. Well, it's a surprise to me that those who once had their own small flocks of sheep grazing here, before these walls, have allowed these changes to happen; but the whole thing is beyond my capacities at the moment – I cannot hope to comprehend it. The first man who, having enclosed a piece of ground, bethought himself of saying, This is mine, and found people simple enough to believe him – he was the founder of civic society. I was right when I wrote that. The hatred I feel, provoked by the ruination of the people through the greed of their lords, the injustice of it, to partition things in this way, without realising the truth: the fruits of the earth belong to us all, and the earth itself belongs to nobody. I spent some time today watching a man build one of the walls – skilled and ponderous work, slow-going, but rhythmic – perhaps if I were stronger, it would be the kind of work I might like to have done, deliberate, methodical, precise. But no. I wouldn't want to be the one who erects the boundaries in the landscape, I would be the one to tear them down, to knock the walls apart.

I will describe the room in which I write. It is a sandstone cave, underneath one of the terraces on the western side of the house. It is small, a few paces in length and breadth. There is a narrow wooden door which faces south. Inside there is a fireplace, a stone bench to the left, some alcoves for reliquaries to the right. A small window facing east looks out, not into the world, but into a corridor in the servants' quarters. No light gets in from outside unless the door is open. The door is rarely open, thanks to the weather. I sit on the stone bench in the alcove, with a candle. In certain conditions the walls are damp to the touch. The fireplace is small and does not give off much heat. If I can't be out walking, I am in my cave. What else? Nothing else in the room. The walls are blank, hewn from the stone; a cold tawny brown. Of course there are many other rooms in the house that would be better suited to other people undertaking the task I am working towards, but none of these rooms would do for me. Nobody has tried this task before: the full honest revelation of their complete natural self. There is no precedent. I could not write it in a more luxurious room: I need the sparse and honest simplicity which this cave offers me. If I am cold, I pull my robe tighter around me. I pull my squirrel cap over my ears. I stamp around the room a little. In summer perhaps I will open the door and let in some fresh air – or perhaps not, perhaps then I will not write at all, I will walk out in the fields and look for more specimens. Davenport has been generous with paper, laying in a vast supply. Mr Walton assures me he can easily obtain more, and any thing else I need. I must pay Davenport for my materials when he visits. I will ask him to sell some of my books, perhaps my etchings. So here I am then, in my cave, holed up in the dark cold damp, and I set my mind back on the sun-filled days of my childhood, the days of vagrancy in the valleys of the Alps, when I set off from Geneva without knowing what would happen, with a certainty that sooner or later I would be put in my rightful place, never suspecting that I would end up here, in a wet and dark cave in a foreign country, alone and friendless, wracked by pains and remorse, persecuted from all sides. No – I exaggerate. I am not friendless: there are those who are kind to me, those that do love me still. But even though I have achieved the state of solitude that I have wanted for so long, I am still inclined to feel pity for my condition. I think back on the last encounters I had in Switzerland, when I was uprooted from my happiness on the Île de St Pierre, the only place I have truly felt myself to be content, in the midst of persecution, and I reflect on what I have lost, what I have given up to come here, to sit in the dark and cold, and I feel that I must mourn the life that I have lost, as well as the life I never had. I think back to the Île de St Pierre and dwell on my happiness there in the midst of it all. I wonder how the rabbit colony I started on the island is doing. Taking the small creatures across the water in a small rowing boat, the rabbits shaking, terrified of Sultan, who crouched at my feet looking equally as scared of them – a delightful and charmed memory from perhaps the place on this earth where I could most feasibly have been quite happy. I must do something to seriously occupy myself in the days on which the weather prevents me from going outside. I have been thinking about Annecy, cherry-picking as a youth, the first flirtations, my mock-chivalric behaviour, ridiculous, the abundance of the earth, the richness of early summer – bright skies, verdant grasses which feel somehow too green to be real, unbearable to look at for too long – the feeling of excitement and possibility; genuine hope, uncontaminated by mere relief – the optimism of my youth expressed in the glory of the sunlight breaking through the canopy in a day in June in the Alps – so distant from the miserable gloom which lingers in this country, dark and wet.

This afternoon a visit from the parson. He walked here across the empty fields. He came alone. A tall man, thin, stooping slightly. The servants thought it a notable event, and tried to communicate its significance to me by moving with more haste than usual. I suppose he ministers to some of their needs. We sat by the fire and were served, inevitably, with some tea. He did not speak my language. I do not speak his. We sat in silence, uncomfortable in each other's presence. I wanted to ask if Davenport had sent him, perhaps to check up on me. I tried to ask. The parson looked up at me, encouragingly, smiling, glad for a beginning to the conversation, relieved to be on comfortable ground. I struggled with the words. Not just with the language, of which I still know almost nothing, and the little I do know fading by the day, but with the exact question I was trying to ask. Was I being spied upon? Was the parson here out of idle curiosity? A sense of duty to his faith?: "Yes, oh yes, indeed, indeed." The parson's irrepressible good humour manifested itself as a need to agree. He did not know what exactly he was agreeing to. I did not know what this answer committed him to. He smiled placidly back at me, then looked away, down into his cup. He stirred his tea. He sighed. He looked back up at me, and then away quickly. I sat, observing this stranger, a growing anxiety in my breast, half irritated at having been disturbed, half relieved not to be writing, worried about my duties of hospitality, wishing to be alone. What was Thérèse doing? She would not be able to speak to the parson either. What would he make of her? What did he make of me? He looked as if to speak, then seemed to think better of it, returning to his tea. The fire crackled. The silence of the house lay around us. Wind in the chimney. It was mid-afternoon. I heard a door close somewhere distant. The same crows outside again. Caw, caw, caw. I felt myself trapped in this room. The tea in my cup was cold. I coughed. The parson said something I didn't understand. I looked at him with a questioning glance. Here followed something incomprehensible. I smiled at him and nodded. What else could I do? He must have thought me a fool. I looked out of the window. The same endless grey bank of cloud, the same drizzle. I longed to be outside, in the woods. How long we sat there, separate from each other, forced in on ourselves, I don't know. It felt interminable. Eventually he stood up. He must have warmed himself enough at the fire. I stood up. We both smiled, embarrassed. I felt no fondness for him. What did he feel for me? He said something else in his language, which I didn't understand. Again, I smiled at him. I bowed my head. He stretched out his hand, which I took, and we walked to the door, which he shut behind him. I returned to the fireplace. In the corridors I could hear him talking to one of the male servants, but I couldn't understand what they said to each other. A loud laugh from one of them, I couldn't tell which. I had not heard the parson laugh during our meeting. For that matter I had not knowingly heard any of the male servants here laugh. I was filled with anxious melancholy. Perhaps this parson had been kind and sincere in his visit, hoping to encourage a new resident in his parish, wanting to disburden himself of his own miseries and strains. Perhaps he was a parson-natur-alist, of which this country produces so many, and we could have discussed our botany, we could share the pleasures of long walks together, returning to this room with our specimens, from out of the drizzle, comparing notes over some wine, talking long into the night, tentatively at first, but soon in full flow, opening our hearts to one another. Perhaps this parson might have been the friend I have been seeking. Probably not, but perhaps. Would he come again? I had given him no sign that he would be welcome, but he would not be unwelcome. What was the laugh about? Noth-ing funny had happened in the room while we had been talking. And once again the familiar gloom settled over me, the feeling of separation, the loneliness to which I felt condemned, as if I had missed another chance to really commune with another person, to reveal myself in full to them and to be taken as I was. I looked into the fire and thought of my life as a whole, as a series of missed opportunities and wrong turns, false steps, the incorrect handling of situations which I had misread or misunderstood. I had trusted people and been mistreated. I had not trusted people and mistreated them in my turn. This parson was the last in a long line of errors I had made through being ignorant or awkward or churlish. I looked into the fire and wanted to weep. What was I doing in this miserable place? Why had I come here? I had spoken to nobody for weeks. Other than Thérèse, who had not wanted to come here at all. I had wanted to be alone, and now I was alone. Except for Thérèse and the servants. But at the first flickering hope of a friend I had allowed myself to expect more. I had wanted to like the parson, but had been distrustful too. When would Davenport come? And when he did come, would he reveal himself to me, in his full open honesty? After his dissimulation over the payment for the carriage, I doubted it. I felt the old aches once again. It was time to return to my desk, I needed to get on with my writing, to take my mind out of this hole and to go back to the gentler times of my life, back to when I could trust in full innocence, when I could express myself clearly and honestly, with love, when I could hope for a life of ease and pleasure to unfold in front of me. A life so different from my current position in this dismal pit. My life in the sun and forests by Annecy, in the care and loving embrace of Maman, in the first place that I felt understood and truly, fleetingly, happy.

Davenport arrived a few days ago with my letters, at long last. What should have been a welcome event was complicated by the fact that the majority of the envelopes he brought with him appear to have been opened and hastily resealed. This had been a problem in London – not always, but I found that Hume was often keen to learn the contents of my letters, one way or another, and more than once they were delivered to me with a burn mark around the seal, implying careless efforts at hiding the subterfuge. Again, much of my recent correspondence has come to me through the hands of the good David. I can only believe that he has been reading these letters too. He says he is my friend, but what kind of friend behaves in such a way? What does he hope to learn from reading my letters? Perhaps he scans them looking for flattering allusions to his own person and his recent noble behaviour in finding sanctuary for me here. But he should know that looking amongst private papers that do not belong to you, that are not meant for your eyes, is a guaranteed way to learn something unpleasant about yourself. But more than any thing, this recent insult confirms my growing sense that I am not quite safe even here from the schemes that have pursued me, and that I must especially protect my manuscript. A number of events and actions have given me reason to begin to truly distrust Hume, and in my solitude here it is easy enough to work over these slights and upsets again and again, rubbing them raw, instead of letting them heal and moving on in our friendship. That he is reading my letters is one circumstance among many other smaller signs that cause my trust in him to fray. Otherwise, I am glad Davenport is here. He is a good host and a gentle companion; I begin to feel the loneliness slide off me, the beginning of the thaw. I might show him some of the work I have been engaged on since arriving. But he is hard to read: silent, passive, reserved, agreeable but remote, like talking to a glacier – no hope there for mutual confidences. I have met few people as emotionally impregnable as he is. How much of this emotional distance is the staid comfort of the wealthy Englishman, how much personality, how much distrust from whatever it is that David has been telling him about me? Already Davenport has introduced me to Granville, a wealthy man who has recently bought Calwick Abbey, but a few miles distant, a large house near a lake with some wonderful gardens about it. He is fluent in my language and musically inclined, was friends with a great composer, and has an excellent harpsichord in his house, much better than the spinet I have at my disposal. It is a relief to find someone here who I can talk to. Of course Davenport is a fine man who has been extremely kind to me, but he is aloof. Granville's heart seems more open. And he is accompanied by his niece, Mary, twenty years old and a true delight. I sang them some of my own airs, accompanying myself, and she was clearly moved by me. She has expressed an interest in botany but says she knows very little – I have offered to teach her the small amount I can retain myself. My heart stirs for her, but I must remember my position here. Granville has also offered to make further introductions, to other botanising acquaintances of his, a duchess of somewhere, and I am glad for the opportunity to expand my circle wherever possible, especially if the expansion consists of people to whom it is possible to speak freely, for once. My hopes of finding a good and honest friend among the people here wax and wane like the moon: I am tentative with everyone, almost bashful, awkward in the small society I have found here, from fear of ruining things again.

A long walk with Sultan today, to Ilam and back. The wind still painful but for once blue skies lay open above me and the birds were tentatively singing. Out of the wind it was nearly warm, and I felt once more that I was beginning to thaw – life was restored to my body as I climbed upon the dark moors, shot through with glimpses of black peat. There are so many sheep here; it is almost unbearable at times, the constant droning of them as you approach yet another drystone wall marking a recent boundary. It's difficult to keep Sultan close, since the livestock represent a rare glimmer of excitement for him, but I worry about an altercation with a yeoman, or some other inhabitant, and so I have to be stern with my friend. More than once on this walk today someone came across me while I was in a compromising position: bent or squatting to examine a plant, or with my arm wedged up to my shoulder between some boulders, trying to scrape off some moss. I am no further with my botany – nothing sticks in my mind. But it is still a delight to me, more for the chain of associations which arise from the activity than any thing else. When I wander through the woods or along the banks of the stream, I am reminded of the woods and waters of my earlier days, and I remember the pleasures of solitude; I forget my persecution at the hands of men, I forget their hate, their scorn, their insults and the malign deeds they perform, I remember the happy days of my childhood, I am transported to the peaceful places in which I spent my youth, and the good and simple people with whom I spent those years. I enjoy my innocent pleasures all over again, and despite suffering the worst fate ever endured by a mortal being, I can momentarily become happy again, out with the plants, the same leaves, the same fronds, stems, flowers; they can transport me better than any book or musical work. At one point earlier, I was lying down and leaning over a rocky outcrop halfway up a slope, trying to get close to a particularly interesting-looking specimen of lichen, which I could not quite recognise or identify, when I heard soft footsteps and whispers behind me. I hauled myself up and saw two children, a boy and a girl, poorly dressed and barefoot, gazing at me in rapt horror. One had a finger in its mouth and a weeping sore on its forehead. I tried to smile and beckon them closer, but as soon as I opened my mouth to greet them, they began to shriek, and fled down the hill, back the way I had just come. I didn't understand, but I suppose my attire must have worried them. Perhaps there is a rumour floating around regarding what exactly it is that I do on these walks, since I imagine to the eyes of the local peasantry it can't appear that I'm doing any thing useful, or meaningful, and perhaps even that I might be engaged in something malign. By now I have walked out across these hills a good number of times, and I still feel no closer to understanding them or their layout – they seem to stretch on unendingly, small villages dotted about almost at random, places which typically consist of no more than a few small dwellings inhabited by malnourished labourers. I have only ventured into the closest town once so far – it holds no attraction for me whatsoever. There are people there who have asked to make my acquaintance but I have not responded to their overtures. Though there is one young aristocrat who seems as if he might be companionable: Brooke Boothby, who Granville has recommended to me. He flits back and forth between England and France, but spends his time on the Continent at a military academy in Caen and has no connections with the philosophers in Paris. I am told that he has read my writings carefully, which naturally makes me hesitate in trusting too much in the prospect of his friendship, but perhaps soon I will invite him to visit me regardless.

I showed Davenport a few pages of the manuscript. He read them in silence while I sat uneasily, trying not to watch his progress. After a long while he finished and put them to one side. He said that he thought them excellent, a wonderful style, and that it appeared that I had gone further in the direction of introspection and self-analysis than any one he had read, further than Montaigne, further than Augustine, yes, this was a real accomplishment in his eyes, remarkable, he would have huge supplies of paper and ink sent to the house so that I could continue on this work unimpeded by any conditions or lack. I thanked him for his kindness, his sympathy, for understanding, then hesitated a little, before explaining to him that the work I am engaged upon is not, despite his interpretation of it, a work of inward-facing soul-searching, not just a series of recollections, or a personal evaluation, not a way of coming to terms with myself, or of reaching a new degree of comprehension of my own character, my personality, my history, no, what I am doing is more imperative than any of that, less related to the petty business of trying to know oneself. I already know myself, I told him. My work has a different purpose: it is a justification, an honest account of my personality and my behaviour, a defence mounted against the unending insinuation and constant public attacks against me; my work is a way for me to present my own interpretation of the events which had happened to me, a way of settling the egregious falsehoods about me which have been spread, to show the world – not myself, nor God – who exactly I was and how I had acted: honesty, in its fullness, was what I sought, not for its own sake, not as a good in itself, not as the mere history of one particular individual, however interesting I might personally be, but as a piece of evidence in the course of litigation which my life had become. Since my reputation was inevitably going to be destroyed by my enemies while I still lived, it would be degraded even further after my death unless I myself left some strong justification and defence of myself, before it was too late for me to put pen to paper. I may be mistreated in this life, I said to Davenport, but this work would guarantee that, at least for those who cared to read it, the truth of my life and my innocence would exist in some form, accessible to open hearts. This was why I had to go deeper than the others before me, why I had to begin an enterprise which was completely original – it would be wrong to present myself as completely innocent in all matters, as though I were free from sin and error, and that is the reason why I was forced to work over all of my worst and most wretched acts in such detail: I needed to show myself exactly as I was, no better and no worse, and that process necessarily involved a closer attention to the worse side of my behaviour, so as to emphasise the disproportionate level of retribution I have suffered at the hands of my enemies, who I have in fact not wronged at all. I told him that if my work seemed different from the other writers he had read, it was merely because there was no tone or style available to me that would unravel the immense chaos of feelings, so diverse, so contradictory, often so vile and sometimes so sublime, by which I was ceaselessly agitated; it was necessary for me to invent a new language to express all this, a mode of writing that was as new as my project was, one which could see no imitation or equal. Davenport heard this all out with his usual placidity. I don't know if he understood what I meant to say, but he did not argue with me, merely repeated his promise to have a large supply of writing materials sent to the house, and said that I should of course let him know if I wanted any thing else. I had tried to explain myself, but once again felt that I had failed, or had been misunderstood. I couldn't express myself to Davenport, I couldn't share my desire, or the imperative I felt: to cast one's mind back into the first experiences, and to try, alone, to recollect every detail, no matter how shameful or degrading, to disentangle the knots of resistance and forgetfulness, to try to re-order the events which appear to me now only as fragmentary and incoherent, glimpses or flashes of clarity in a dark and unfathomable sea of lost moments – I cannot remember every external event, but it seems that every feeling I have ever had is still there, somewhere in the archive of my mind, and the task ahead of me is to delve into those feelings in order to reveal to myself what their cause might have been. It is of no interest

to me to recount my life as a series of simple actions –
what happened when, where, in what order; no, I am
interested in revealing the movements of my heart in
all their shades and hues – joy, sadness, childish over-
excitement, dark despair, gloom; I feel that I have
always retained a large part of the attitudes of the
child I once was – if I am not quite an adult now, even
now, at this advanced age, it is because I was forced to
behave like one too early in life; I have kept something
of both states, and perhaps this is why I am so easily
moved. All of my former wounds are still open to me,
waiting to reveal themselves, like the body of the victim of scurvy, whose old scars all show themselves in
the advanced stage of his illness.

For a while I slept easily here, for the first few weeks
after our arrival. But recent articles in the newspapers
that reach here have disrupted the equanimity I was
beginning to feel. I know that I cannot trust Hume at
all now, that he is in league with my enemies, with
those in France that seek to damage my name and
reputation. I feel anxious, and with the mental distress, my body has started to collapse again. The
insomnia that plagued me for many years is back. Up
all last night again, writing – not through any desire to
put pen to paper, or through any urge to continue with
the work, but because the pain in my bladder makes
sleep impossible. Thérèse removed the catheter with
her usual care, but for some reason it was more painful than usual, and there was some blood. No urine at

all for more than a day now; the pressure is unbearable. I have to walk, or hobble, back and forth in front of the fire, which must still be lit, even though we are now approaching days that should be accompanied by the warmth of spring, if not summer. I compose sentences in my head, to distract myself from the agony, and then I rush to the paper to set down a few words when a phrase is fully formed. As soon as the ink touches the paper, whatever was in my mind seems to evaporate, dissipating into nothing, and I can only scratch out something weakly approximate to the sentence I had contrived just a minute ago, never any thing too long before the discomfort of sitting gets too much and I have to stand up again, pacing back and forth once more. The progress is excruciating. I worry that the soft tip of the rod of the catheter has detached itself inside my urethra again and is calcifying into a stone – the pain is close to that of the infections I have had in the past. I suspect when the time comes and I am able to pass water, I will be pissing gravel. Beyond this physical pain, though: on some days I feel as though everything were shrouded in a thick bank of cloud; impenetrable, murky, opaque. I sit out in the cave and try to think back to the defining hours of my life, but nothing comes to me – it is as if I have always been here, in this small room carved out of the rock, with my papers and a few books, a small fire burning, two candles to keep away the gloom – nothing before, nothing to come, no passage of time, no ageing, no communication; all is blank, null. I stare at the brown wall and I do not think. Then, after some time in this attitude, either some recollection begins to poke through into my consciousness, or I give up, extinguishing the candles and starting out again across the heathlands.

A letter, alleging to be from the King of Prussia, has appeared in the newspapers – both in Paris and London. It is false, I know that for certain. But who is responsible for the forgery? Who would write such a thing? It is surely one of the philosophers, one of my enemies. Not Diderot, but perhaps Grimm, or more likely d'Alembert. Voltaire, perhaps. It has his style. I read it over and over. Its contents follow me on my walks. The insult contained in it is cruel, unnecessary. It is short. I have it nearly by memory now. Thérèse laughed when she read it but tried to stifle her mirth. A laceration. I am not angry, but hurt – confused – sad. The letter reads:

You have renounced Geneva, your native soil. You have been driven from Switzerland, a country of which you have made such boast in your writings. In France you are outlawed: come then to me. I admire your talents, and amuse myself with your reveries – on which, by the way, you bestow too much time and attention. It is high time to grow prudent and happy; you have made yourself sufficiently talked of for singularities little becoming a truly great man. Show your enemies that you have sometimes common sense, for that will vex them without hurting you. My dominions offer you a peaceful retreat. I desire to do you good, and will do it, if you can but think it such. But if you are determined to refuse my assistance, you may expect me to say not a word of this to anyone. If you persist in striving to discover new misfortunes, choose such as you like best. I am a King, and can make you as miserable as you wish. And something that will surely not happen to you vis-à-vis your enemies: I will cease to persecute you when you cease to glory in your own persecution.

The King of Prussia, who through his connection with Lord Keith, my protector and dearest friend, my father, has been nothing but kind to me – he offered me asylum, which I turned down to come to England – he would of course not deign to write such an insulting letter to as inconsequential a person as myself. Why do I attract the ire of these people, why can I not escape their hatred, their slings, even in this remote isolation I have taken myself off to?

This morning the weather was clear. A mild breeze, nothing severe. I set off along the banks of the stream with my eyes open wide. The stone walls here had revealed themselves to be loaded with plants I could not recognise. I had spent the previous evening painfully making my way through one of the books on botany I had brought with me, focusing in particular on the mosses and the lichens. My eyes tire quickly these days, and my memory is fading. So I must have read the same passages, the same pages, over and over again for hours, hoping that some part of the information would gain a footing in my mind. As I walked along the stream I noted the spot where I had previously seen saxifrage alpina. At first glance I almost thought it a fresh discovery, but then remembered having the same experience at the same spot two days earlier. Though the weather was worse then. The failing of my memory is painful to me when I think about it as something abstract, as a condition of my body's disintegration, but at least it has its mercies: I no longer recall all of the slights I have received, and I am capable of experiencing old pleasures as if for the first time. I followed the stream some way, until it reached an old bridge in the same brown-grey stone as everything else in this place. Standing on the other bank of the stream was an enormously fat man in the guise of a fellow botanist. He was dressed moderately well and was leaning over, examining a small plant which I could not see from my position. He looked at me furtively, then looked back to the plant. I approached. I felt nervous that this might be someone sent to observe me by Hume, towards whom I feel increasingly afraid, and who I begin to suspect must be seeking new ways to track my movements, limited though they are. But I am lonely, I craved conversation, and I thought that it might be pleasant to talk about the plants with someone. Perhaps this man could help me with my lichens, the easy identification of which still escapes me. Davenport and Granville had both made their promises about introductions to botanically inclined friends, who they assured me were trustworthy, but these meetings have not yet been forthcoming. So I decided to address the stranger. Of course, I used my own language, having no other. I asked if he were a botanist. He was – he looked very gratified to be addressed as such and responded quite comfortably in my language, without a strong accent. Ah! I drew closer to him, to see what he was looking at, but I could not identify the plant. I didn't want to spoil this new friendship by immediately displaying ignorance and so I asked him to walk on with me a short way. He would. He would be delighted to, in fact. Good. Good. We made some vague remarks about the weather's improvement of late. I asked if he knew the area well. If he lived far. Not too well, but not too far, he said. He did not ask me about my own situation. I thought this odd. I assumed my presence was conspicuous enough that it might require no further explanation. Word had got out. People knew that a foreigner with peculiar dress was in the region; enough of them had come to gawp at me. I was not too suspicious of my new friend, my brother botanist. The man seemed fairly innocuous, with the air of amiable softness that many men of his bulk have. Though of course David has a similar build and does not have the same softness about him at all. No, David has a kind of bovine hostility surrounding him: equal parts blandness and threat. My new friend seemed a little nervous, anxious about something, fizzing with a kind of energy like a child with a secret. The path narrowed a little ahead of us, and because of his girth I was forced to walk behind him. I could no longer see his face as he told me about the unusual length of the winter this year; I replied that I was well aware of how long it had been. I started to tell him about my bladder complaint, but decided to leave it until we were better acquainted. A lull in the conversation followed. I asked the stranger his name. He hesitated and then gave it: Erasmus. Erasmus! I cried, delighted. A wonderful name. He turned to face me, his size blocking the way. He bowed, and repeated his name, adding his surname, and the town where he lived. I knew the name already – I had been invited to meet this man but had refused to do so. The scales fell from my eyes: this was indeed one of Hume's associates, one of the local philosophers, involved in one of the unbearable learned societies that every bog or pit in this country seems to be teeming with. David was incorrigible, inescapable. That I should be spied on here, in this way! By this oaf! It seemed David's contrivance knew no limits. My walk was ruined. I shouted at this Erasmus to leave me alone, that I knew what he was about, that he should not bother me again, and I turned on my heel and stormed back to the house at once, locking myself away, refusing even to see Davenport.

The days pass feverishly at the moment. I spend all of my time at my desk, working on the endless letters I am obliged to write, turning over the events of the past few months, from the period in Môtiers, through the

Île de Saint-Pierre, the flight from Switzerland, through Savoy to Strasbourg, up to Paris after deliberating over whether or not to go to Berlin and Prussia, then from Paris to London with Hume, then my journey here and the first few months of isolation before Davenport arrived. I have to get it all straight, I need to lay it out before me clearly. Davenport's arrival was welcome at first, the company of a sympathetic friend was something I felt keenly lacking, and his appearance seemed to bring with it a shift in the weather, from the leaden and interminable winter to the first days of summer, almost as if spring hadn't taken place at all – one day the earth was as if dead, and the next the trees are budding, the nightingales sing, nature opens up with a yawning sigh. Then she shuts again for some weeks, but soon starts to tentatively reveal herself again. The weather has continued to be pleasant over the past few weeks, and I would in other circumstances be out walking more than I am able to at the moment. Instead I find myself trapped inside, my mind spinning, imprisoned by the snare into which I have been led. My letters, entrusted to Davenport's care, so as to save money on the postage, have all clearly been read, opened and hastily resealed. When I considered refusing the receipt of all mail whatsoever here, Hume argued that if I did so then the letters addressed to me would be read by the authorities, who would subsequently be aware of all of my plans and movements; this would be inadvisable, he thought, and I agreed, wanting to preserve what little was left of my privacy as far as possible. After all, there are still arrest warrants out for me on the Continent. But I did not expect that in following this advice I would be subject to invasive acts of this kind by the person who alleged to be my friend. It is clear that he is monitoring my letters. That is one thing. This question of the pension raises another problem: Hume's scheme with Davenport to persuade the King to pay me an annuity. It puts me in a difficult position, impossible, since I have turned down similar sinecures from other European monarchs, and I do not want it to be made public that I accept the favours of monarchy. I need the money; but it seems tainted somehow, orchestrated in such a way as to ensure that both options – acceptance or refusal – are wrong, and the situation will only serve to provide the public with greater opportunity to scorn me, and more ammunition for the press to use against me. There is a concerted effort to make me appear ridiculous and immoral in this country, and I cannot account for the change in tone that has taken place in the newspaper articles which refer to me over the short time I have been a resident here. I have done nothing, have published nothing, have appeared nowhere, spoken to nobody, I have tried to remove myself from the eye of the public, but still find my name in the papers which come to the house, and rarely is my name presented with any terms of endearment or admiration or respect. Why is this? Why can I not be left to my own devices here? I have been hounded out of so many places that I would quite happily recant everything I've ever written, if only I could guarantee that I would be left alone and forgotten about by the world at large. I have introduced a cipher into my letters and reduced the number of my correspondents significantly, but I have also been at work on a campaign of defence, making sure my friends and my enemies all know that I am cognisant of the attacks against me, of the scheming that goes on behind my back. I am full of anger at the moment, a zealous and burning sensation runs through my body, a certainty of having been wronged. But lurking behind this is a morose sadness that I have once again attracted so much disdain, so much maliciousness, so many attacks on my name and reputation. I feel despondent after the hours spent producing these letters in my defence. Then I try to go out into the country, but if it is late when I finish my letters and the night is setting in, then I must remain indoors – and I pick up the pen again and get to work on my confessions, I set my mind in the happy period before I knew what the attention of the world felt like, before I had tasted injustice to the extent that I encounter it nowadays. To plunge back into the state of mind I had as a child, in my first tastes of freedom I savoured when I fled my home city, abandoning the apprenticeship I had despised, and started to drift through the Savoy landscapes, completely unaware of the path on which I was embarking, wandering without any intention, doing more or less as I pleased – these memories are a relief from the feelings of arid bitterness which make the notes of the emotional scale I range up and down in my daily life here. It isn't easy to account for how the process of recollection can ease my current unhappiness. On the one hand, perhaps it's simply a reminder that, well, at least I was happy once – perhaps – but it's something more than this – it's an accounting for myself, a way of retracing the passage from one state of mind to another, trying to keep track of the elements of myself which have remained constant since my first days, the parts of my character that have been fixed and permanent throughout it all, to recognise the continuities of my life, so as to begin to understand how exactly I came to be in the situation in which I now find myself. It is an active reconstruction, and a close examination and admission of my past behaviour and my failings, as a way of trying to understand the position I am now forced to assume. Less distraction, more penance.

My friendships have hardened and turned into antagonisms; the people who claimed to love me best have become my most aggressive pursuers. I think about the Plutarch I read on my father's knee as a small boy in his workshop, until the early hours and the singing of the lark woke us from our rapt fascination. Not just his Lives, but his moral essays: these were my education, I never spent a day in school but instead gleaned what knowledge I could from wherever it could be found. Plutarch taught me that one can profit from one's enemies, because their attentions lead one into a life of careful circumspection and an unassailable and exact regime – I could profit from the assaults upon my person and the depths of misery into which the betrayals cast me by keeping my own heart and conscience pure and clear – honesty, truth, confessing my missteps, my sins, my errors, my transgressions, my lies, the acts I was most ashamed of, what else, my falsehoods – if I lay myself bare then what ammunition would my tormentors have to use against me? I have committed no crime in the eyes of man or God, nothing too serious, but there were shameful incidents in my past which I felt like a wound. Perhaps if I could relive those moments, or confess them, show them to the world, whether in my lifetime or after my death, I would eventually find the peace which my enemies refused to allow me. In this way I could profit from them, and follow the lessons of my first and best teacher. But that boyhood reading of the philosopher did not prepare me for the pain caused by the enmity I have encountered since. Plutarch embraces having enemies, but to me it is an unbearable torment, because they pursue me endlessly, they plot and conspire against me, they raise mobs to stone my houses, they turn the common people – who I love dearly and, after all, belong to – against me; they falsify, they lie, they gossip, they malign me unceasingly and across borders and across seas. Even here, in this miserable waste of a country, even here they can reach me and torment me – they engineer new ways to besmirch my name and undermine me, to infringe upon my freedom, to humiliate me. They recruit all, they act in league with each other, forgetting about their own hatred of each other, united in their resentment of me, the most disparate individuals with nothing in common except a desperate passion for destroying my peace of mind – they plot and scheme and leave me with just enough sense of liberty that I feel its limits more keenly. Hume is not even the worst of them; he is, of course, only a small element of the larger and deeper scheme which has been concocted against me, fermenting and spilling over on the Continent during the last few decades, the plot dreamt up by the philosophers in Paris or Geneva, those false former friends who seek only to make a name for themselves among the society they pretend to criticise while in fact only seeking its favours, those who care nothing for the truth, advancing spurious falsehoods under the guise of enlightenment – hypocrites who once clasped me to their hearts and called me brother, but who abandoned me and now only mention my name for the pleasure of hearing the scornful laugh which follows from all the lips in the fashionable salons and dining rooms in capital cities. I will never go back to them, even if they were to come on their knees to ask my forgiveness – they have hurt me too deeply with their false friendships. David, who I thought the most generous and kindest of men, turns out to share a house with the son of Tronchin, that quack doctor who has been my enemy for years. That alone I could forgive, but I learn that David is also an acolyte of the Encyclopédistes – his grievance over not being recognised here as the genius he thinks himself to be has led him to seek flattery abroad, and he has found it among the smirking hypocrites of Paris. How I could have trusted him, how I could have opened my heart to him, embraced him, loved him, when he was always planning merely to use me to add to his own fame, to show me off like a performing ape captured in the jungle, who can discourse and play the harpsichord and sing in polite company and who can laugh at a comedy and weep at a tragedy, but who ultimately, when the candle is extinguished and everyone is in bed, is still merely a comical beast who has managed to dress itself in some ridiculous foreign outfit and pretended to be civilised for a day – all for the entertainment of the cultivated philistines who habituate society. Yes, it will surely add to his fame, his having trapped and captured an exotic and unusual specimen like me, to have bundled him off to the middle of nowhere for a while. But perhaps I am unreasonable and getting carried away. I could have gone elsewhere, but I chose to come here. I had other offers: Prussia, Poland, Corsica. I chose David, I chose his preferred friendship, and I chose England. I longed for the liberty I had heard people enjoyed here. I have not seen those liberties, either here or in London. I don't know if they exist anywhere, except perhaps among the nobility here, who do as they please. But is that freedom? Not for me. Freedom is being left alone and supporting yourself through independence and work: the freedom enjoyed by the citizen of Geneva, the citizen which I was, which I might still be had it not been for this inescapable plot which smothers me. The experiences of peaceful enjoyment which I had in my youth, with Maman in the countryside, those were my truest encounters with freedom – the freedom to waste my time, to daydream and be idle, to lie in the grass and do very little, to walk by a stream or a lake, to gaze at the reflections playing on the water, to know nothing, to read nothing, not even to botanise, but to let the plants exist on their own, by themselves, for their own purposes; to do nothing, like an animal, free from the demands and poisonous corruptions of the society to which I am doomed to belong.

It is the silence of my enemies that torments me here, combined with the great reduction in letters I receive from friends. It was my own decision to refuse the mail here, and I thought it a good one, but now I know that all letters addressed to me reach my hands already read by my enemies, that they are a key element in this plot against me, the conspiracy to cut off all communication between me and the Continent, I begin to regret my decision. It seems that I send an unending stream of letters out to the world. I am constantly writing one or another, but it is as though months drag by without my hearing any thing from any one. I am wrapped in silence, from which I can only infer the worst; my imagination fixed on the smallest signs, constructing the most developed interpretations, at first out of a kind of idle fancy which I don't quite believe myself, but then these ideas increasingly become concrete, certain, distinct notions which I cannot refute. I persuade myself. I am trapped in this prison, one, I accept, which is partly of my own making; I hear nothing and I know nothing. Meanwhile my enemies are free to spread falsehoods and calumny about me out in the world, of which I have no part: they communicate freely, while my tongue must remain silent, my hands bound and fettered. I vibrate between a feeling of euphoric righteousness and a deep melancholy. I am in the right, I acclaim myself, I have acted bravely, almost heroically. But I am alone, I have been betrayed, I thought those that loved me would be loyal to me, but they have turned out to hate me too, like all the rest. It is a real strain, and my heart is wretched. I feel sick, exhausted. It is all I can do to put down words on the page in whatever order they come to mind, in the hope that through this process I will gradually inch closer to some resolution. I walk and my mind gets stuck, circling around in the loops of half-finished phrases and unclear ideas, rotating on the same spot with no forward motion. Stuck. I despair. I feel disgusted with work and with life; I wish that I could find one sentence which could express my sentiments exactly and precisely and which would make the truth finally manifest. If only I could formulate it, as though it were an incantation or a spell, which once uttered would transform the world, turn it from a wretched place of interminable wrongness into something less unbearable. I cannot express my feelings with any clarity because they exist only vaguely and imprecisely in my body, their translation into thought is inaccurate and disquieting. Even this attempt to express the wrongness I feel is, in its turn, wrong, unsatisfying, upsetting in its confused result. I understand nothing, and I am full of nauseous dread. I continue with the cipher in my letters, and have told even more of my friends to stop writing to me. Du Peyrou writes, suggesting a new edition of my works, but I am not interested; he also suggests that I might get in touch with a man named Cerjat, a countryman of mine, who lives in some eastern corner of this country, who is well out of all intrigue and might provide some service for me. Perhaps, perhaps. I am lonely, and feel my friends slipping away. I don't know if I have the energy for new ones now. I have had no word from any one else. If only Lord Keith would write. I long to see him soon; he is one of the few men who truly understands me, who welcomes what others see as eccentricities. Maybe I should go to live with him in Scotland, but the weather there must be far worse than it is here, and my body will not bear it if I put it through any more extreme conditions.

I find myself constantly revisiting in my mind the first night with David, turning it over again and again, revolving my thoughts around the phrase I heard him shout more than once that evening. I could not tell whether he was awake or asleep. It seems to me, on reflection, that he must have been asleep, that he was giving voice to some true, genuine feeling that he would have been unable to utter in the daylight, he would not have been able to bring himself to admit it, it would have immediately revealed his malicious attitude towards me: in sleep he could not help himself from expressing the satisfaction he felt on achieving his deeply held desire. At the time I had taken his expression to be a benign intimation of his careful generosity towards me, but during the long, sleepless nights here it has increasingly begun to appear to me in a sinister light and I cannot leave it alone; I keep returning to the moment, picking at it, even though it leaves me feeling disquieted and unhappy; I heard it as an expression of a triumphant conqueror, rather than of someone showing solicitous tenderness. What did he say? "I have him." He said that in my language: *Je tiens Jean-Jacques Rousseau.* An expression of threat. I heard the words clearly; the more I think about it the more certain I am. We were at Senlis, on the way to Calais. It was night, we were sharing a room. He cried out, with extreme vehemence, the phrase I have recorded. *I have him.* Yes, that night at Senlis comes back to me in a sinister light. When we landed at Dover I threw my arms around his neck and wept, he had saved me, but he responded mildly, and perhaps seemed a little embarrassed by the situation. Embarrassed! And again, at London, he had fixed his ominous gaze upon me, dry, burning, mocking, prolonged – hard to describe, inscrutable, both ferocious and bland at the same time – as if he were trying to appear placid despite some horrible and monstrous passion. I glared back at him at first, but could not hold out. I was wracked by an involuntary shudder and turned my gaze to the floor. I felt guilty that I was unable to trust this kind, gentle, tender-hearted, generous man who had saved me from persecution, who had put himself through no small trouble to bring me here, where I was safe – or at least on my way to safety. The tears welled in my eyes. I felt a deep revulsion towards my own behaviour. I was wretched. I threw myself on his neck and embraced him tightly and, suffocating with sobs and tears, I cried brokenly: "No, no, the good David is no traitor! If he was not the best of men, he would have to be the worst!" He returned my embrace with more of his phlegmatic politeness, patting me on the back with little taps, and comforting me in the tone of a grandfather tending to an infant. "There now. There, my dear sir. Now now. Oh, my dear sir." Cold caresses – he would not be moved by my feelings of repentance. His response was not enough to calm my suspicions. I have him. What did he mean by those words? Why did he utter them in such a vehement tone? I still don't know if he was awake or asleep. The good David, large and bland, his empty gaze fixed in the corner of the room, then suddenly turned on my own face, smiling gently, gazing, unblinking, as if expecting something, impossible to read his expression – as if he is sitting with either a completely empty mind or with a mind full of malicious schemes. He is not an evil man, not wicked, no, I'm sure. But if he is not the best of mankind then he must surely be the worst. In London he was eager to read the letters I received; he was jealous of my correspondence. Did he hope that by introducing me to society there he was going to receive some reflected fame? Some glory? He can have it. How could he be innocent of what I suspect of him? He is in league with the others. But I can't imagine what he hopes to gain from keeping me in his power – I am worth nothing to any one else, I value myself highly only because nobody else will. The matter of the pension from the King is another trap: how can I accept something that is not freely and spontaneously given? If I refuse, I will appear proud, scornful, and I will lose the money which I quite urgently need. But if I accept, then I will appear arrogant, thinking that I deserve to be paid merely to be kept alive, and I will be thrown back into the role of supplicant, of lackey, of mendicant, which I have spent so much effort trying to escape. Why can these people not see that all I value is my independence? Or perhaps they do see that, and it is exactly why they seek to compromise it. More sleepless nights this past week. I feel as though I have not slept well for months. All night I try feverishly to relive my only moments of happiness, and I work my way through every false step and wrong turn I have taken, filling my heart with yearning for the life I might have led if only I had been able to behave differently, to feel less, to think more, to be other than that which I am. But it's a pointless wish – I am as I was made – I have always suffered from too keen an emotional capacity and too sluggish a mind. I sit and write for hours, it comes in no order – I try to start at the beginning and hope to finish at the end, in a straight line, but the pattern of my thinking is irregular, my movements are uneven, I can't remember it all, I oscillate, I repeat myself, I get stuck in quagmires of self-pity and shame and regret – but despite that I am happy when I pen these anecdotes, put them to paper, when in my mind I can be back in the valleys and forests, walking with no sense of direction, no hope for the future, no company, just reveries, fantasies, dreams of heroics, my entire life open, ahead of me – yes, even though the purity of that happiness I felt then has long since faded and now seems irrecoverable, I don't mind, not really, since it is enough for me to know that I was happy once – I was happy only when I thought I might eventually find a place in the world which acknowledged me, recognised me, welcomed me. The pursuit of that dream has led me only to misery, but the dream itself was once a source of the greatest joy I have experienced.

When I first met David I thought there might be something about him that I would struggle with. Something in his manner grated – possibly some slight evasiveness, inattention, uncertainty: it was unclear whether or not our relationship would be genuinely friendly or whether it would be based merely on our positions in the shared world, the so-called Republic of Letters. He was always unforthcoming, withdrawn, a little reserved and distracted in most things, but would occasionally express a keen alacrity when certain mundane topics were raised – the cost of postage, the use of his seal, his receipt of my letters to forward on to me – things like that sparked enthusiasm in him, but when I expressed myself and my heart openly to him, when I revealed the depths of my feeling, the extent of my gratitude for his help in my search for asylum, then he was cold, distant, icy. I don't want someone who is as withdrawn and unpredictable as he is for a friend: I need constancy, reliability. But we were thrown under the glare of public attention almost instantly, our natural feelings for each other barely had time to develop before we were obliged to appear linked to each other's name, to be seen together – yes, obliged; it was a relationship of obligation, and we both were forced to act in ways that ran counter to our usual dispositions. Was I harsh in my suspicions of him? I might have been, and I have occasionally regretted my actions, but I have since been proven right in my assessment of his dishonesty and callousness. To threaten to publish an account of our quarrel, to make our private letters public, to defend himself by attacking and humiliating me, in the open, casting me in the light of a hysterical and lying malcontent, ungrateful, paranoid – this is dismal behaviour on his part. All night long I turn it around, try to think how I might have acted to avoid all this, and I can see no point at which I might have been other than I am. I have behaved with honour, and a clear mind, I have pointed out hypocrisy and deception, and my reward for acting virtuously is to be humiliated and shunned.

Last night, in a fit of desperation, I sat at my desk and wrote for hours straight, a hundred pages perhaps, I tore through years of my life in a kind of fury, longing to have them finished with and behind me. If I write so much now it is only from the desire to be done with it, to stop the wheels from turning, to finally reach the point at which the pen can drop from my hands and I can say: Enough. The moment, long anticipated, of silence, of peace, of the end of this compulsion, to have bridged the gap with words, and finally to find the reconciliation I have been seeking for so long. The sooner this is finished, the sooner this scratching is all over, well, the better; the sooner I can stop, the sooner the disgust I feel might be lightened, the sooner the rancour inside me might be assuaged.

High summer in the woods now, the canopy above my head is thick and opaque, casting only small fragments of sunlight onto the floor; the air is cool and still among the trees, but out in the fields the sun is hot, and dark clouds start to form on the horizon. The dog days. My mind feels unsteady and the obsessive focus on David's behaviour has kept me awake for what seems like days. I thought I had freed myself of him and his machinations, but things still churn away despite my intentions. Davenport tries to distract me but I soon feel that I am suffocating in his company and have to set off by myself. But in the woods I do not find the pleasure or distraction that I hope for; I feel myself observed, I see faces peering out from between branches, see people slinking out of sight just ahead, find myself looking into the higher limbs of the trees to check whether anybody is hiding there, observing me. I know that most likely I imagine these things, but at moments it is as though the world has cast off its usual appearance and I have stepped into some unrecognisable zone where the normal journey from sensation to certainty is disturbed. I doubt my experiences but can't quite fully convince myself of my doubt. Everyone I pass is suspicious – I eye them warily and they reciprocate my gaze. Either they are paid spies, or more likely – I know – they are bothered by the unusual clothes I wear and don't know what to make of my activities out on the hills. On my desk at the house there is a stack of half-finished letters, on which I could not bear to write another word. I doubt all of my friends now too, I don't know who I can write to openly, without fear that they will betray my confidence, either by passing on any information I send to my enemies directly, or indirectly, or by turning their back on me, like so many already have. I worry too about repeating myself in my letters, about harping on about the same things without remembering that I have already written to everyone the exact same sentences that I am putting down for the fourth or fifth time. The solution has been to keep copies of all letters I send, to copy all outgoing correspondence, which of course doubles my exertions and makes my task of self-defence seem unending, a constant reiteration of the same things, the same wounds prised open again and again. And each repetition solidifies my doubts more certainly. It is an abysmal state to be in, and I can see no path out of the predicament, other than through writing a single, final summary, lengthy and complete, laying out the whole plot against me as I perceive it, and directly accusing David and his accomplices, in writing, in the eye of the public if need be. The world must know of the mistreatment I have experienced, if only so that the few rare good and true men on this earth might be able to learn the truth about the behaviour of those that would call themselves philosophers.

Let me revolve it all again: it is night, in David's rooms, in London, before I arrived here. Outside it is raining. The room is illuminated by a few candles and a small fire. I have gone to remonstrate with him about his collusion in trying to organise my transportation here without my paying for it myself. I must retain my independence, I remind him, and even if the offer is a generous one, it is also a deception: honesty, especially in financial matters, is more important to me than generosity. I tell David this. He responds in his typical manner, trying to brush the issue aside, all politeness and good humour. Good. I must try to be clear now about what happens. I lapse into silence and we sit facing each other. The light is insufficient, my eyes suffer. His gaze is fixed on my face. He has his hands clasped over his stomach, he leans back slightly, he fixes his eyes on me. What does he express in that look? Malice? Contempt? Satisfaction? I cannot read him; he makes himself closed to me. Hostile. I try to look back at him with the same expression, but cannot bear the tension, so I get up and start pacing the room. He continues to look at me in the same way, but still neither of us speaks. What is going through his mind? What is going through mine? Here things become opaque – my recollection of my thoughts becomes hazy – I only know that I am at this point afraid of Hume and that I suspect him. I could not say what exactly I suspect him of. Luring me here, being an accomplice of my enemies abroad? I don't know. I start to remonstrate with myself now: David has been good to me; he has gone through a lot of trouble for me; he is kind, a good man, one of the very best; I am the one that is reprehensible, wretched, for even beginning to suspect that I could have been mistreated by a kind, good man such as my friend David is; I am ungrateful; what must he think of my behaviour, coming here to attack him, to demean our friendship, his generosity, bringing up this unseemly, grotesque, false accusation of mine? I pace back and forth in the room, my mind reeling. His eyes are still on me when I turn to face him. Eventually it starts to feel too much for me to hold in, the tears start to come – I always cry so easily – and I throw myself on his neck, sobbing. I spill out my heart to him, I confess what I suspected him of, I accuse myself, naming in detail the baseness of which I believe myself to be guilty, I tell him that he deserves better than me, then I can't say any more, my tears take over completely, I cling to him, abject. He pats me on the back, gently: "Oh, my good sir! What, my good sir?" Platitudes – platitudes only; he cannot bring himself to express his own feelings, if indeed he has any. He remains cold, closed. His inadequate response manages to stop my tears, but I sense something shift in a corner of my mind; a suspicion confirmed about him, a feeling hardening, a wound forming a scab. Why did he not fully embrace me? Why did we not weep together? I have shown him my tenderness towards him, my appreciation of him, more than once now; I have thrown myself on his neck and wept, but he never joins me – he always looks embarrassed, ashamed of himself, ashamed of me, of the situation, uncomfortable, awkward, he doesn't know how to respond. His reserve implies a guilty mind – otherwise why wouldn't he be moved by as pathetic a sight as that which I present to him, on my knees, clutching at him and gasping between sobs, asking for his forgiveness like a child? – I am on my knees, when in fact it is he who has been in the wrong and should be apologising to me. The more I dwell on it, the harder my heart becomes against him, and I am certain that he has in fact succeeded in luring me into a trap from which I cannot hope to escape.

A bright summer day, sultry, the trees enormous in the fullness of their foliage. It is hot for once, the sun blazes in the sky. There is no breeze and I am soon soaked in sweat as I climb up the rocks to collect my specimens. I have done with David. The matter is resolved for the time being; I have sent him a long letter, informing him that I am aware of his intentions, that his behaviour has not fooled me, that he is in league with my enemies, with Grimm, with Diderot, d'Alembert, Voltaire, all of them. He seeks acclaim from the frivolous monde, and he thinks he will get it by joining in with their persecutions of an innocent man: childish bullies. Well, good luck to them. They did not account for the possibility of my retaliation; they expect me to be quiet, mild, and accept the barbs they throw at me. I will cut off contact with David and not think of him any longer. Finally, finally, I can allow myself to enjoy this place.

*

Sir,

I am indisposed, and little in a situation to write; but you require an explanation, and it must be given you: it was your own fault you had it not long since; but you did not desire it, and I was therefore silent: at present you do desire it, and so I have sent it. It will be a long one, for which I am very sorry; but I have much to say, and would put an end to the subject at once.

As I live retired from the world, I am ignorant of what passes in it. I have no party, no associates, no intrigues; I am told nothing, and I know only what I feel. But care has been taken to make me severely feel; I know that well. The first concern of those who engage in bad designs is to secure themselves from legal proofs of detection: it would not be very advisable to seek a remedy against them at law. The innate conviction of the heart admits of another kind of proof, which influences the sentiments of honest men. You well know the basis of my own sentiments.

You ask me, with great confidence, to name your accuser. That accuser, Sir, is the only man in the world whose testimony I should admit against you; it is yourself. I shall give myself up without fear or reserve to the natural frankness of my disposition; being an enemy to every kind of artifice, I shall speak with the same freedom as if you were an indifferent person, on whom I placed all that confidence which I no longer have in you. I will give you a history of the emotions of my heart, and of what produced them; while, speaking of Mr Hume in the third person, I shall make yourself the judge of what I ought to think of him. Notwithstanding the length of my letter, I shall pursue no other order than that of my ideas, beginning with the premises, and ending with the demonstration.

I left Switzerland, wearied out by the barbarous treatment I had undergone; but which affected only my personal security, while my honour was safe. I was going, as my heart directed me, to join Lord Marshal, Keith; when I received at Strasburg a most affectionate invitation from Mr Hume, to go over with him to England; where he promised me the most agreeable reception, and more tranquillity than I have met with. I hesitated some time between my old friend and my new one; in this I was wrong. I preferred the latter, and in this was even more so. But the desire of visiting in person a celebrated nation, of which I had heard both so much good and so much ill, prevailed.

Assured I could not lose George Keith, I was flattered with the acquisition of David Hume. His great merit, extraordinary abilities, and established probity of character, made me desire the annexing of his friendship to that with which I was honoured by his illustrious countryman. Besides, I gloried not a little in setting an example to men of letters, in a sincere union between two men so different in their principles.

Before, I had received an invitation from the King of Prussia, and my Lord Marshal, undetermined about the place of my retreat, I had desired, and obtained by the interest of my friends, a passport from the Court of France. I made use of this, and went to Paris to join Mr Hume. He saw, and perhaps saw too much of, the favourable reception I met with from a great Prince, and I will venture to say, of the public. I yielded, as it was my duty, though with reluctance, to that éclat; concluding how far it must excite the envy of my enemies. At the same time, I saw with pleasure the regard which the public entertained for Mr Hume, sensibly increasing throughout Paris, on account of the good work he had undertaken with respect to me. Doubtless he was affected too; but I know not if it was in the same manner as I was.

We set out with one of my friends, who came to England almost entirely on my account. When we were landed at Dover, transported with the thoughts of having set foot in this land of liberty, under the conduct of so celebrated a person, I threw my arms round his neck, and pressed him to my heart, without speaking a syllable; bathing his cheeks, as I kissed them, with tears sufficiently expressive. This was not the only, and not the most remarkable instance I have given him of the effusions of a heart as full of sensibility as mine. I know not what he does with his recollection of these instances, when he does recollect them; but I have a notion they must be sometimes troublesome to him.

On our arrival in London, we were mightily caressed and entertained: all ranks of people eagerly pressing to give me marks of their benevolence and esteem. Mr Hume presented me politely to everybody; and it was natural for me to ascribe to him, as I did, the best part of my good reception. My heart was full of him. I spoke in his praise to every one, I wrote to the same purpose to all my friends; my attachment to him gathering every day new strength, while his attachment to me appeared likewise the most affectionate; of which he frequently gave me instances that touched me extremely. His causing my portrait to be painted, however, was not of the number. This seemed to me to carry with it too much the affectation of popularity, and had an air of ostentation which by no means pleased me. All this, however, might have been easily excusable, had Mr Hume been a man apt to throw away his money, or had a gallery of pictures with the portraits of his friends. After all, I freely confess that, on this head, I may be in the wrong.

But what appears to me an act of friendship and generosity the most undoubted and estimable, in a word, the most worthy of Mr Hume, was the care he took to solicit for me, of his own accord, a pension from the King; to which most assuredly I had no right to aspire. As I was a witness to the zeal he exerted in that affair, I was greatly affected with it. Nothing could flatter me more than a piece of service of that nature; not merely for the sake of interest; for, too much attached, perhaps, to what I actually possess, I am not capable of desiring what I have not, and as I am able to subsist on my labour and the assistance of my friends, I covet nothing more. But the honour of receiving testimonies of the goodness, I will not say of so great a monarch, but of so good a father, so good a husband, so good a master, so good a friend, and above all, so worthy a man, was sensibly affecting: and when I considered farther, that the minister who had obtained for me this favour, was a living instance of that probity which of all others is the most important to mankind, and at the same time hardly ever met with in the only character wherein it can be useful, I could not check the emotions of my pride, at having for my benefactors three men, who of all the world I could most desire to have my friends. Thus, so far from refusing the pension offered me, I only made one condition necessary for my acceptance; this was the consent of a person, whom I could not, without neglecting my duty, fail to consult.

Being honoured with the civilities of all the world, I endeavoured to make a proper return. In the meantime, my bad state of health, and being accustomed to live in the country, made my residence in town very disagreeable. Immediately country houses presented themselves in plenty; I had my choice of all the counties of England. Mr Hume took the trouble to receive these proposals, and to represent them to me; accompanying me to two or three in the neighbouring counties. I hesitated a good while in my choice, and he increased the difficulty of determination.

At length, I fixed on this place, and immediately Mr Hume settled the affair; all difficulties vanished, and I departed; arriving presently at this solitary, convenient, and agreeable habitation; where the owner of the house provides every thing, and nothing is wanting. I became tranquil, independent; and this seemed to be the wished for moment, when all my misfortunes should have an end. On the contrary, it was now they began; misfortunes more cruel than any I had yet experienced.

Hitherto I have spoken in the fullness of my heart, and to do justice, with the greatest pleasure, to the good offices of Mr Hume. I wish to Heaven that what remains for me to say were of the same nature! It would never give me pain to speak what would redound to his honour; nor is it proper to set a value on benefits till one is accused of ingratitude; which is the case at present. I will venture to make one obser- vation, therefore, which renders it necessary. In estimating the services of Mr Hume, by the time and the pains they took him up, they were of an infinite value, and that still more from the goodwill displayed in their performance; but for the actual service they were of to me, it was much more in appearance than reality. I did not come over to beg my bread in Eng- land; I brought the means of subsistence with me. I came merely to seek an asylum in a country which is open to every stranger without distinction. I was, besides, not so totally unknown as that, if I had arrived alone, I should have wanted either assistance or service. If some persons have sought my acquaintance for the sake of Mr Hume, others have sought it for my own. Thus when Mr Davenport, for example, was so kind as to offer my present retreat, it was not for the sake of Mr Hume, whom he did not know, and whom he saw only in order to desire him to make me his obliging proposal. So that when Mr Hume endeavours to alienate from me this worthy man, he takes that from me which he did not give me. All the good that hath been done me, would have been done me nearly the same without him, and perhaps better; but the evil would not have been done me at all: for why should I have enemies in England? Why are those enemies all the friends of Mr Hume? Who could have excited their enmity against me? It certainly was not I; who knew nothing of them, nor ever saw them in my life: I should not have had a single enemy had I come to England alone.

I have hitherto dwelt upon public and notorious facts; which from their own nature, and my acknowledgment, have made the greatest impression. Those which are to follow are particular and secret, at least in their cause, and all possible measures have been taken to keep the knowledge of them from the public; but as they are well known to the person interested, they will not have the less influence toward his own conviction.

A very short time after our arrival in London, I observed an absurd change in the minds of the people regarding me, which soon became very apparent.

Before I arrived in England, there was not a nation in Europe in which I had a greater reputation than here, nor, I will venture to say, was held in greater estimation. The public papers were full of encomiums on me, and a general outcry prevailed on my persecutors. This was the case at my arrival, which was published in the newspapers with triumph; England prided itself in affording me refuge, and justly gloried on that occasion in its laws and government: when, all of a sudden, without the least assignable cause, the tone was changed; and that so speedily and totally, that of all the caprices of the public, never was known any thing more surprising. The signal was given in a certain Magazine, equally full of follies and falsehoods, in which the author, being well informed, or pretending to be so, gives me out for the son of a musician. From this time, I was constantly spoken of in print in a very equivocal or slighting manner. Every thing that had been published concerning my misfortunes was misrepresented, altered, or placed in a wrong light, and always as much as possible to my disadvantage. So far was anybody from speaking of the reception I met with at Paris, and which had made but too much noise, it was not generally supposed that I had dared appear in that city; even one of Mr Hume's friends being very much surprised when I told him I came through it.

Accustomed as I had been too much to the inconstancy of the public to be affected by this instance of it, I could not help being astonished, however, at a change, so very sudden and general, that not one of those who had so much praised me in my absence, appeared, now I was present, to think even of my existence. I thought it something very odd that, immediately after the return of Mr Hume, who had so much credit in London, with so much influence over the booksellers and men of letters, and such great connections with them, his presence should produce an effect so contrary to what might have been expected; that among so many writers of every kind, not one of his friends should show himself to be mine; while it was easy to be seen that those who spoke of him were not his enemies, since, in noticing his public character, they reported that I had come through France under his protection, and by favour of a passport which he had obtained of the court; nay, they almost went so far as to insinuate, that I came over in his retinue, and at his expense. All this was of little signification, and was only singular; but what was much more so, was, that his friends changed their tone with me as much as the public. I shall always take a pleasure in saying that they were still equally solicitous to serve me, and that they exerted themselves greatly in my favour; but so far were they from shewing me the same respect, particularly the gentleman at whose house we alighted on our arrival, that he accompanied all his actions with discourse so rude, and sometimes so insulting, that one would have thought he had taken an occasion to oblige me, merely to have a right to express his contempt.

His brother, who was at first very polite and obliging, altered his behaviour with so little reserve, that he would hardly deign to speak a single word to me even in their own house, in return to a civil salutation, or to pay any of those civilities which are usually paid in like circumstances to strangers. Nothing new had happened, however, except the arrival of J-J Rousseau and David Hume: and certainly the cause of these alterations did not come from me, unless indeed showing too great a portion of simplicity, discretion, and modesty is the cause of offence in England. As to Mr Hume, he was so far from assuming such a disgusting tone, that he gave into the other extreme. I have always looked upon flatterers with an eye of suspicion: and he was so full of all kinds of flattery, that he even obliged me, when I could bear it no longer, to tell him my sentiments on that head. His behaviour was such as to render few words necessary, yet I could have wished he had substituted, in the room of such gross encomiums, sometimes the language of a friend; but I never found any thing in his language which tasted of true friendship, not even in his manner of speaking of me to others in my presence. One would have thought that, in endeavouring to procure me patrons, he strove to deprive me of their goodwill; that he sought rather to have me assisted than loved; and I have been sometimes surprised at the rude turn he has given to my behaviour before people who might not unreasonably have taken offence at it. I shall give an example of what I mean. Mr Pennick of the Museum, a friend of my Lord Keith's, and minister of a parish where I was solicited to reside, came to see me. Mr Hume made my excuses, while I myself was present, for not having paid him a visit. Doctor Matty, said he, invited us on Thursday to the Museum, where Mr Rousseau should have seen you; but he chose rather to go with Mrs Garrick to the play: we could not do both the same day. You will confess, Sir, this was a strange method of recommending me to Mr Pennick.

I know not what Mr Hume might say in private of me to his acquaintance, but nothing was more extraordinary than their behaviour to me, even by his own confession, and even often through his own means. Although my purse was not empty, and I needed not that of any other person – which he very well knew – any one would have thought I was come over to subsist on the charity of the public, and that nothing more was to be done than to give me alms in such a manner as to save me a little confusion. I must admit that this constant and insolent piece of affectation was one of those things which made me averse to reside in London. This certainly was not the footing on which any man should have been introduced in England, had there been a design of procuring him ever so little respect. This display of charity, however, may admit of a more favourable interpretation, and I consent it should. To proceed.

In Paris a fictitious letter from the King of Prussia was published, addressed to me, and replete with the most cruel malignity. I learned with surprise that it was one Mr Walpole, a friend of Mr Hume's, who was the editor; I asked him if it were true; in answer to which question, he only asked me, from whom I had the information. A moment before he had given me a card for this same Mr Walpole, written to engage him to bring over such papers as related to me from Paris, and which I wanted to have by a safe hand.

I was informed that the son of that quack Tronchin, my most mortal enemy, was not only the friend of Mr Hume, and under his protection, but that they both lodged in the same house together; and when Mr Hume found that I knew it, he imparted it in confidence; assuring me at the same time, that the son was by no means like the father. I lodged a few nights myself, together with my gouvernante, in the same house; and by the air and manner with which we were received by the landladies, who are his friends, I judged in what manner either Mr Hume, or that man, who, as he said, is by no means like his father, must have spoken to them both of her and me.

All these facts put together, combined with a certain appearance of things on the whole, insensibly gave me a feeling of uneasiness – which I rejected with horror. In the meantime, I found the letters I wrote did not come readily to hand; those I received had often been opened; and all went through the hands of Mr Hume. If at any time any one escaped him, he could not conceal his eagerness to see it. One evening in particular I remember a very remarkable circumstance of this kind, that greatly struck me. As we were sitting one evening, after supper, silent by the fireside, I caught his eyes intently fixed on mine, as indeed happened very often; and that in a manner of which it is very difficult to give an idea; at that time he gave me a steadfast, piercing look, mixed with a sneer, which greatly disturbed me. To get rid of the embarrassment I lay under, I endeavoured to look full at him in my turn; but, in fixing my eyes against his, I felt the most inexpressible terror, and was obliged soon to turn them away. The speech and physiognomy of the good David is that of an honest man; but where – great God! – did this good man borrow those eyes he fixes so sternly and unaccountably on his friends!

The impression of this look remained with me, and gave me much uneasiness. My trouble increased even to a degree of fainting; and if I had not been relieved by an effusion of tears, I would have suffocated. Immediately after this I was seized with the most violent remorse; I even despised myself; until at length, in a transport which I still remember with delight, I sprang on his neck, embraced him eagerly; while almost choked with sobbing, and bathed in tears, I cried out, in broken accents, "No, no, David Hume cannot be treacherous; if he be not the best of men, he must be the basest of mankind!" David Hume politely returned my embraces, and gently tapping me on the back, repeated several times, in a good-natured and easy tone, "Why, what my dear Sir!

Nay, my dear Sir ! Oh! my dear Sir!" He said nothing more. I felt my heart yearn within me. We went to bed; and I set out the next day for the country.

Arrived at this agreeable asylum, to which I have travelled so far in search of repose, I ought to find it in a retired, convenient, and pleasant habitation; the master of which, a man of understanding and worth, spares for nothing to render it agreeable to me. But what repose can be tasted in life, when the heart is agitated? Afflicted with the most cruel uncertainty, and ignorant what to think of a man whom I ought to love and esteem, I endeavoured to get rid of that fatal doubt, in placing confidence in my benefactor. For, wherefore, from what unaccountable caprice should be shown so much apparent zeal for my happiness, and at the same time, the entertainment of secret designs against my honour. Among the several observations that had disturbed me, each fact was in itself of no great moment; it was their concurrence that was surprising; yet I thought, perhaps, that Mr Hume, informed of other facts of which I was ignorant, could have given me a satisfactory solution to them, had we been able to come to an explanation. The only thing that was inexplicable was that he refused to come to such an explanation, which both his honour and his friendship rendered equally necessary. I saw very well there was something in the affair which I did not comprehend, and which I earnestly wished to know. Before I came to an absolute decision with regard to his personality, I desired to make another effort, and to try to recover him if he had permitted himself to be seduced by my enemies, or, in short, to prevail on him to explain himself one way or other. Accordingly I wrote him a letter, which he ought to have found very natural, if he were guilty; but very extraordinary, if he were innocent. For what could be more extraordinary than a letter full of gratitude for his services, and at the same time, of distrust of his sentiments; and in which, placing in a manner his actions on one side, and his sentiments on the other, instead of speaking of the proofs of friendship he had given me, I desired him to love me, for the good he had done me? I did not take the precaution to preserve a copy of this letter; but as he has it, let him produce it: whoever reads it, shall see therein a man labouring under a secret trouble which he is desirous of expressing, and is afraid to do it, and any reader will, I am certain, be curious to know what kind of éclaircissement it produced, especially after the preceding scene. None! Absolutely none at all! Mr Hume contented himself, in his answer, with only speaking of the obliging offices Mr Davenport had proposed to do for me. As for the rest, he said not a word of the principal subject of my letter, nor of the situation of my heart, of whose distress he could not be ignorant. I was more struck with this silence than I had been with his phlegm during our last conversation. In this I was wrong: this silence was very natural after the other and was no more than I ought to have expected. For when one has ventured to declare to a man's face, "I am tempted to believe you a traitor", and he has not the curiosity to ask you why, it may be depended on that he will never have any such curiosity as long as he lives, and it is easy to judge him from these slight indications.

After the receipt of his letter, which was long delayed, I determined at length to write to him no more. Soon after, everything served to confirm me in the resolution to break off all further correspondence with him. Curious to the last degree concerning the minutest circumstance of my affairs, he was not content to learn them from me directly, in our frequent conversations, but, as I learned, he never let slip an opportunity of being alone with my gouvernante, to interrogate her even importunately concerning my occupations, my resources, my friends, acquaintances, their names, situations, place of abode, and all this after setting out with telling her he was well acquainted with all of my connections. Nay, with the most jesuitical address, he would ask the same questions of us separately. One ought undoubtedly to interest one's self in the affairs of a friend; but one ought to be satisfied with what he thinks proper to let us know of them, particularly when people are as frank and ingenuous as I am. Indeed – all this petty inquisitiveness is very little becoming a philosopher.

About the same time I received two other letters which had been opened. The one from Mr Boswell, the seal of which was so loose and disfigured, that Mr Davenport, when he received it, remarked the same to Mr Hume's servant. The other was from Mr d'Ivernois, in Mr Hume's packet, which had been sealed up again by means of a hot iron, which, awkwardly applied, had burnt the paper round the impression. On this, I wrote to Mr Davenport to desire him to take charge of all the letters which might be sent for me, and to trust none of them in anybody's hands, under any pretext whatever. I know not whether Mr Davenport, who certainly was far from thinking that precaution was to be observed with regard to Mr Hume, showed him my letter or not, but this I know – that Mr Hume had all the reason in the world to think he had forfeited my confidence, and that he proceeded nevertheless in his usual manner, without troubling himself about the recovery of it.

But what was to become of me, when I saw, in the public papers, the pretended letter of the King of Prussia, which I had never before seen, that fictitious letter, printed in French and English, given for genuine, even with the signature of the King, and in which I knew the pen of Mr d'Alembert as certainly as if I had seen him write it? In a moment a ray of light discovered to me the secret cause of that sudden change which I had observed in the public respecting me, and I saw that the plot which was put in execution at London had been first laid in Paris.

Mr d'Alembert, another intimate friend of Mr Hume's, had been long since my secret enemy, and lay in watch for opportunities to injure me without exposing himself. He was the only person, among the men of letters, of my old acquaintance who did not come to see me or send their civilities during my last passage through Paris. I knew his disposition, but I gave myself very little trouble about it, contenting myself with advising my friends of it occasionally. I remember that being asked about him one day by Mr Hume, who afterwards asked my gouvernante the same question, I told him that Mr d'Alembert was a cunning, artful man. He contradicted me with a warmth that surprised me; not knowing then that they stood so well with each other, and that it was his own cause he defended. The perusal of the false letter above mentioned alarmed me a good deal, when, perceiving that I had been brought over to England in consequence of a project which began to be put in execution – of the end of which I was ignorant – I felt the danger without knowing what to guard against, or on whom to rely. I then recollected four terrifying words Mr Hume had made use of, and of which I shall speak hereafter. What could be thought of a paper in which my misfortunes were imputed to me as a crime, which tended, in the midst of my distress, to deprive me of all compassion, and, to render its effects still more cruel, pretended to have been written by a Prince who had afforded me protection? What could I divine would be the consequence of such a beginning? The people in England read the public papers, and are in no ways prepossessed in favour of foreigners. Even a coat, cut in a different fashion from their own, is sufficient to excite *a prejudice against them. What then had not a poor stranger to expect in his rural walks, the only pleasures of his life, when the good people in the neighbourhood were once thoroughly persuaded he was fond of being persecuted and pelted? Doubtless they would be ready enough to contribute to his favourite amusement. But my concern, my profound and cruel concern, the bitterest indeed I ever felt, did not arise from the danger to which I was personally exposed. I had braved too many others to be much moved with that. The treachery of a false friend to which I had fallen a prey was the circumstance that filled my too susceptible heart with deadly sorrow. In the impetuosity of its first emotions, of which I never yet was master, and of which my enemies have artfully taken the advantage, I wrote several letters full of disorder, in which I did not disguise either my anxiety or indignation.*

I have, Sir, so many things to mention, that I forget half of them by the way. For instance, a certain narrative in form of a letter, concerning my manner of living at Montmorency, was given by the booksellers to Mr Hume, who showed it to me. I agreed to its being printed, and Mr Hume undertook the care of its edition; but it never appeared. Again, I had brought over with me a copy of the letters of Mr du Peyrou, containing a relation of the treatment I had received at Neufchatel. I gave them into the hands of the same bookseller to have them translated and reprinted. Mr Hume charged himself with the care of them; but they never appeared. The supposititious let-

ter of the King of Prussia, and its translation, had no sooner made their appearance, than I immediately comprehended why the other pieces had been suppressed, and I wrote as much to the booksellers. I wrote several other letters also, which probably were handed about London; until at length I employed the credit of a man of quality and merit, to insert a declaration of the imposture in the public papers. In this declaration I concealed no part of my extreme concern, and nor did I in the least disguise the cause.

Hitherto Mr Hume seems to have walked in darkness. You will soon see him appear in open day, and act without disguise. Nothing more is necessary, in our behaviour toward cunning people, than to act ingenuously – sooner or later they will infallibly betray themselves.

When this pretended letter from the King of Prussia was first published in London, Mr Hume, who certainly knew that it was fictitious – as I had told him so – said nothing of the matter, did not write to me, but was totally silent; and did not even think of making any declaration of the truth in favour of his absent friend. It answered his purpose better to let the report take its course, as he did.

Mr Hume having been my conductor into England, he was of course in a manner my patron and protector. If it were but natural in him to undertake my defence, it was to less so that, when I had a public protestation to make, I should have addressed myself to him. Having already ceased writing to him, however, I had no mind to renew our correspondence. I addressed myself therefore to another person. The first slap on the face I gave my patron. He felt nothing of it.

In saying the letter was fabricated at Paris, it was of very little consequence to me whether it was understood particularly of Mr d'Alembert, or of Mr Walpole, whose name he borrowed on the occasion. But in adding that, what afflicted and tore my heart was, the impostor had got his accomplices in England; I expressed myself very clearly to their friend, who was in London, and who wanted to pass for my friend too. For certainly he was the only person in England whose hatred could afflict and rend my heart. This was the second slap of the face I gave my patron. He did not feel, however, yet.

On the contrary, he maliciously pretended that my affliction arose solely from the publication of the above letter, in order to make me pass for a man who was excessively affected by satire. Whether I am vain or not, it is certain that I was mortally afflicted; he knew it, and yet he did not write me a single word. This affectionate friend, who had so much at heart the filling of my purse, gave himself no trouble to think my heart was bleeding with sorrow.

Another piece appeared soon after, in the same papers, by the author of the former, and still if possible more cruel; in which the writer could not disguise his rage at the reception I met with at Paris. This however did not affect me; it told me nothing new. Mere libels may take their course without giving me any emotion; and the inconstant public may amuse themselves as long as they please with the subject. It is not an affair of conspirators, who, bent on the destruction of my honest fame, are determined by some means or other to effect it. It was necessary to change the battery.

The affair of the pension was not determined. It was not difficult, however, for Mr Hume to obtain, from the humanity of the minister and the generosity of the King, the favour of its determination. He was required to inform me of it, which he did. This, I must confess, was one of the critical moments of my life. How much did it cost me to do my duty! My preceding engagements, the necessity of shewing a due respect for the goodness of the King, and for that of his minister, together with the desire of displaying how far I was sensible of both; add to these the advantage of being made a little more easy in circumstances in the decline of life, surrounded as I was by enemies and evils; in fine, the embarrassment I was under to find a decent excuse for not accepting a benefit already half accepted; all these together made the necessity of that refusal very difficult and cruel: for necessary it was, or I should have been one of the meanest and basest of mankind to have voluntarily laid myself under an obligation to a man who had betrayed me.

I did my duty, though not without reluctance. I wrote immediately to General Conway, and in the *most civil and respectful manner possible, without giving an absolute refusal, excusing myself from accepting the pension for the present.*

Now, Mr Hume had been the only negotiator of this affair – the only person who had spoken of it. Yet I not only did not give him any answer, though it was he who wrote to me on the subject, but did not even so much as mention him in my letter to General Conway. This was the third slap of the face I gave my patron; which, if he does not feel, it is certainly his own fault – he can feel nothing.

My letter was not clear, nor could it be so to General Conway, who did not know the motives of my refusal; but it was very plain to Mr Hume who knew them but too well. He pretended nevertheless to be deceived as well with regard to the cause of my discontent, as to that of my declining the pension; and, in a letter he wrote me on the occasion, gave me to understand that the King's goodness might be continued towards me, if I should reconsider the affair of the pension. In a word he seemed determined, at all events, to remain still my patron, in spite of my teeth. You will imagine, Sir, he did not expect my answer; and he had none. Much about this time, for I do not know exactly the date, nor is such precision necessary, appeared in the public eye a letter, from Voltaire to me, with an English translation, which still improved on the original. The noble object of this ingenious performance, was to draw on me the hatred and contempt of the people, among whom I was come to reside. I made not the least doubt that my dear patron was one of the instruments of its publication; particularly when I saw that the writer, in endeavouring to alienate from me those who might render my life agreeable, had omitted the name of him who brought me over. He doubtless knew that it was superfluous, and that with regard to him nothing more needed to be said. The omission of his name, so impolitely forgot in this letter, recalled to my mind what Tacitus says of the picture of Brutus, omitted in a funeral solemnity, that is, that every body took notice of it, particularly because it was not there.

Mr Hume was not mentioned; but he lives and converses with people that are mentioned. It is well known his friends are all my enemies; there are abroad such people as Tronchin, d'Alembert, and Voltaire; but it is much worse in London; for here I have no enemies but those who are his friends. For why, indeed, should I have any other! Why should I have even them? What have I done to Lord Littleton, whom I don't even know? What have I done to Mr Walpole, whom I know full as little? What do they know of me, except that I am unhappy, and a friend to their friend Hume? What can he have said to them, for it is only through him they know any thing of me? I can very well imagine that, considering the part he has to play, he does not unmask himself to everybody; for then he would be disguised to nobody. I can very well imagine, that he does not speak of me to General Conway and the Duke of Richmond, as he does in his private conversations with Mr Walpole, and his secret correspondence with Mr d'Alembert; but let any one discover the clue that has been unravelled since my arrival in London, and it will easily be seen whether or not Mr Hume holds the principal thread. At length the moment arrived in which it was thought proper to strike the great blow; the effect of which was prepared for, by a fresh, satirical piece, put in the papers. Had there remained in me the least doubt, it would have been impossible to have harboured it after perusing this piece; as it contained facts unknown to anybody but Mr Hume; exaggerated, it is true, in order to render them odious to the public.

It is said, in this paper, that my door was opened to the rich, and shut to the poor. Pray who knows when my door was open or shut – except Mr Hume, with whom I lived, and by whom everybody was introduced that I saw? I will except one great personage, whom I gladly received without knowing him, and whom I should still have more gladly received if I had known him. It was Mr Hume who told me his name when he was gone; on which information I was really chagrined that, as he deigned to mount up two pair of stairs, he was not received in the first floor. As to the poor, I have nothing to say about the matter. I was constantly desirous of seeing less company; but as I was unwilling to displease any one, I suffered myself to be directed in this affair altogether by Mr Hume, and endeavoured to receive everybody he introduced as well as I could, without distinction, whether rich or poor. It is said in the same piece, that I received my relations very coldly, not to say any thing worse. This general charge relates to my having once received with some indifference the only relation I have, out of Geneva, and that in the presence of Mr Hume. It must necessarily be either Mr Hume or this relation who furnished that piece of intelligence. Now, my cousin, whom I have always known for a friendly relation and a worthy man, is incapable of furnishing materials for public satires against me. Add to this that his situation in life confines him to the conversation of persons in trade, he has no connection with men of letters, or paragraph-writers, and still less with satirists and libellers. So that the article could not come from him. At the worst, can I help imagining that Mr Hume must have endeavoured to take advantage of what he said, and construed it in favour of his own purpose? It is not improper to add, that after my rupture with Mr Hume, I wrote an account of it to my cousin. In fine, it is said in the same paper, that I am apt to change my friends. No great subtlety is necessary to comprehend what this reflection is preparative to.

But let us distinguish facts. I have preserved some very valuable and solid friends for twenty-five to thirty years. I have others whose friendship is of a later date, but no less valuable, and which if I live, I may preserve still longer. I have not found, indeed, the same security in general among those friendships I have made with men of letters. I have for this reason sometimes changed them, and shall always change them, when they appear suspicious; for I am determined never to have friends by way of ceremony; I have them only with a view to shew them my affection.

If ever I was fully and clearly convinced of any thing, I am so convinced that Mr Hume furnished the materials for the above paper.

But what is still more, I have not only that absolute conviction, but it is very clear to me that Mr Hume intended I should: For how can it be supposed that a man of his subtlety should be so imprudent as to expose himself thus, if he had not intended it? What was his design in it? Nothing is more clear than this. It was to raise my resentment to the highest pitch, that he might strike the blow he was preparing to give me with greater éclat. He knew he had nothing more to do than to put me in a passion and I should be guilty of a number of absurdities. We are now arrived at the critical moment which is to shew whether he reasoned well or ill.

It is necessary to have all the presence of mind, all the phlegm and resolution of Mr Hume, to be able to take the part he has taken, after all that has passed between us. In the embarrassment I was under, in writing to General Conway I could make use only of obscure expressions; to which Mr Hume, in his quality as my friend, gave what interpretation he pleased. Supposing therefore, for he knew very well to the contrary, that it was the circumstance of secrecy which gave me uneasiness, he obtained the promise of the General to endeavour to remove it: but before any thing was done, it was previously necessary to know whether I would accept of the pension without that condition, in order not to expose his Majesty to a second refusal.

This was the decisive moment, the end and object of all his labours. An answer was required; he would have it. To prevent effectually indeed my neglect of it, he sent to Mr Davenport a duplicate of his letter to me; and, not content with this precaution, wrote me word, in another billet, that he could not possibly stay any longer in London to serve me. I was giddy with amazement, on reading this note. Never in my life did I meet with any thing so unaccountable.

At length he obtained from me the so much desired answer, and began presently to triumph. In writing to Mr Davenport, he treated me as a monster of brutality and ingratitude. But he wanted to do still more. He thinks his measures well taken; no proof can be made to appear against him. He demands an explanation; he shall have it, and here it is.

That last stroke was a masterpiece. He himself proves everything, and that beyond reply.

I will suppose, though by way of impossibility, that my complaints against Mr Hume never reached his ears; that he knew nothing of them; but was as perfectly ignorant as if he had held no cabal with those who are acquainted with them, but had resided all the while in China. Yet the behaviour passing directly between us; the last striking words, which I said to him in London; the letter which followed replete with fears and anxiety; my persevering silence still more expressive than words; my public and bitter complaints with regard to the letter of Mr d'Alembert; my letter to the Secretary of State, who did not write to me, in answer to that which Mr Hume wrote to me himself, and in which I did not mention him; and in fine my refusal, without deigning to address myself to him, to acquiesce in an affair which he had managed in my favour, with my own privity, and without any opposition on my part: all this must have spoken in a very forcible manner, I will not say to any person of the least sensibility, but to every man of common sense.

Strange that, after I had ceased to correspond with him for three months, when I had made no answer to any of his letters, however important the subject of it, surrounded with both public and private marks of that affliction which his infidelity gave me; a man of so enlightened an understanding, of so penetrating a genius by nature, and so dull by design, should see nothing, hear nothing, feel nothing, be moved at nothing; but, without one word of complaint, justification, or explanation, continue to give me the most pressing marks of his goodwill to serve me, in spite of myself! He wrote to me affectionately, saying that he could not stay any longer in London to do me service, as if we had agreed that he should stay there for that purpose! This blindness, this insensibility, this perseverance, are not found in nature; they must be accounted for, therefore, from other motives. Let us set this behaviour in a still clearer light; for this is the decisive point.

Mr Hume must necessarily have acted in this affair, either as one of the first or last of mankind. There is no medium. It remains to determine which of the two it hath been.

Could Mr Hume, after so many instances of disdain on my part, have still the astonishing generosity as to persevere sincerely to serve me? He knew it was impossible for me to accept his good offices, so long as I entertained for him such sentiments as I had conceived. He had himself avoided an explanation. So that to serve me without justifying himself, would have been to render his services useless; this therefore was no generosity. If he supposed that in such circumstances I should have accepted his services, he must have supposed me to have been an infamous scoundrel. It was then in behalf of a man whom he supposed to be a scoundrel, that he so warmly solicited a pension from his Majesty. Can any thing be supposed more extravagant? But let it be supposed that Mr Hume, constantly pursuing his plan, should only have said to himself, "This is the moment for its execution; for, by pressing Rousseau to accept the pension, he will be reduced either to accept or refuse it. If he accepts it, with the proofs I have in hand against him, I shall be able completely to disgrace him: if he refuses, after having accepted it, he will *have no pretext, but must give a reason for such refusal. This is what I expect; if he accuses me he is ruined."*

If, I say, Mr Hume reasoned with himself in this manner, he did what was consistent with his plan, and in that case very natural; indeed this is the only way in which his conduct in this affair can be explained, for upon any other supposition it is inexplicable: if this be not demonstrable, nothing ever was so. The critical situation to which he had now reduced me, recalled strongly to my mind the four words I mentioned above; and which I heard him say and repeat, at a time when I did not comprehend their full force. It was the first night after our departure from Paris. We slept in the same chamber, when, during the night, I heard him several times cry out with great vehemence, in the French language, Je tiens Jean-Jacques Rousseau. *I know not whether he was awake or asleep.*

The expression was remarkable, coming from a man who is too well acquainted with the French language to be mistaken with regard to the force or choice of words. I took those words however, and I could not then take them other than in a favourable sense: notwithstanding the tone of voice in which they were spoken, which was even less favourable than the expression. It is indeed impossible for me to give any idea of it; but it corresponds exactly with those terrible looks I have before mentioned. At every repetition of them I was seized with a shuddering, a kind of horror I could not resist; though a moment's recollection restored me, and made me smile at my terror. The next day all this was so perfectly obliterated that I did not even once think of it during my stay in London and its neighbourhood. It was not till my arrival in this place, that so many things have contributed to recall these words to mind; and indeed recall them every moment. These words, the tone of which dwells on my heart as if I had but just heard them; those long and fatal looks so frequently cast on me; the patting me on the back, with the repetition of "O, my dear Sir," in answer to my suspicions of his being a traitor: all this affects me to such a degree, after what preceded, that this recollection, had I no other, would be sufficient to prevent any reconciliation or return of confidence between us; not a night indeed passes over my head, but I think I hear, "Rousseau, I have you," ring in my ears as if he had just pronounced them.

Yes, Mr Hume, I know you have me; but only by mere externals: you have me in the public opinion and judgment of mankind. You have my reputation, and perhaps my security, to do with as you will. The general prepossession is in your favour; it will be very easy for you to make me pass for the monster you have begun to represent me; and I already see the barbarous exultation of my implacable enemies. The public will no longer spare me. Without any further examination, everybody is on the side of those who have conferred favours; because each is desirous

to attract the same good offices, by displaying a sens-
ibility of the obligation. I foresee readily the con-
sequences of all this, particularly in the country to
which you have conducted me; and where, being
without friends and an utter stranger to everybody, I
lie almost entirely at your mercy. The sensible part of
mankind, however, will comprehend that I must be so
far from seeking this affair, that nothing more dis-
agreeable or terrible could possibly have happened to
me in my present situation. They will perceive that
nothing but my invincible aversion to all kind of
falsehood, and the possibility of my professing a
regard for a person who had forfeited it, could have
prevented my dissimulation, at a time when it was on
so many accounts my interest. But the sensible part
of mankind are few, nor do they make the greatest
noise in the world.

Yes, Mr Hume, you have me by all the ties of this
life; but you have no power over my probity or my
fortitude, which, being independent either of you or
of mankind, I will preserve in spite of you. Do not
think to frighten me with the fortune that awaits me.
I know the opinions of mankind; I am accustomed to
their injustice, and have learned to care little about it.
If you have taken your resolution, as I have reason to
believe you have, be assured that mine is taken also.
I am feeble indeed in body, but never possessed
greater strength of mind. Mankind may say and do
what they will, it is of little consequence to me. What
is of consequence, however, is, that I should end as I

have begun; that I should continue to preserve my ingenuousness and integrity to the end, whatever may happen; and that I should have no cause to reproach myself either with meanness in adversity, or insolence in prosperity. Whatever disgrace attends, or misfortune threatens me, I am ready to meet them. Though I am to be pitied, I am much less so than you, and all the revenge I shall take on you, is to leave you the tormenting consciousness of being obliged, in spite of yourself, to have some respect for the unfortunate person you have oppressed.

In closing this letter, I am surprised at my having been able to write it. If it were possible to die with grief, every line would have been sufficient to kill me with sorrow. Every circumstance of the affair is equally incomprehensible. Such conduct as yours has been is not in nature: it is contradictory to itself, and yet it is demonstrable to me that it has been such as I conceive. On each side of me there is a bottomless abyss! and I am lost in one or the other.

If you are guilty, I am the most unfortunate of mankind; if you are innocent, I am the most culpable. You even make me desire to be that contemptible object. Yes, the situation to which you see me reduced, prostrate at your feet, crying out for mercy, and doing every thing to obtain it; publishing aloud my own unworthiness, and paying the most explicit homage to your virtues, would be a state of joy and cordial effusion, after the grievous state of restraint and mortification into which you have plunged me. I have but a word more to say. If you are guilty, write to me no more; it would be superfluous, for certainly you could not deceive me. If you are innocent, justify yourself. I know my duty, I love, and shall always love it, however difficult and severe. There is no state of abjection that a heart, not formed for it, may not recover from. Once again I say, if you are innocent, deign to justify yourself; if you are not, adieu for ever.

*

How BEAUTIFUL the unfolding of the ferns is – I stood and watched the dappled sunlight in the woods, the gentle opening of the fronds happening so slowly in front of me that I could hardly see it, but I focused intently: a slow almost creaking movement, followed by a quick snapping finish; the soil was warm and pungent and I felt myself finally beginning to warm up after the harshness of the winter, opening out after the malice of the past few months – almost calm, for once, out there, away from my desk.

I have received word that Hume will publish our correspondence, in a pamphlet with his remarks and justifications, as well as some letters from his cronies and accomplices. Good. Let the world see how I have been wronged. Those with honest hearts will see the truth in my letters. I have been mistreated. The false pretences under which our supposed friendship was formed, the depth of his perfidy – this will be made clear by the publication. I still continue to revolve it all again. The looks, his coldness, the letters he opened and read. His betrayal. His cowardice. He is responsible for the serious shift against me in the opinion of the newspapers: what other explanation for that could there be? I have told him I am aware of his machinations but I have not heard any more from him directly. I take this as a tacit admittance of his guilt. Maybe the plot against me culminates in this, for now at least. I am out of the world. I will soon be dead anyway, and thankfully away from any state of being where others can injure me. My own manuscript will vindicate me in the eyes of the world – or at least in the eyes of any true man in it. Why should we build our happiness on the opinions of others, when we can find it in our own hearts? I don't care about the opinions of my former friends in Paris and Geneva, or for the moods of the journalists in London – their scorn doesn't affect me in the least. But what does affect me is the practical steps they have taken to obstruct me and to keep me unfree: opening and reading my letters, not even bothering to reseal them properly, preventing me from living unaccosted in solitude, spying on my movements, placing guards about the country. They leave me with the semblance of liberty – apparently I can go where I please – yes, as far away even as Dovedale or Ashbourne or the Manifold Valley; how lucky I am to have such freedom of movement. I chose to come here rather than remain a moment longer in the rankness of London, but I didn't realise that I would be subject to constant observation even in this most remote place. My encounter with the fat man from Lichfield, sent by the good David to gather information, to observe my movements, to try to lull me into a friendship, to remind me that I am under close watch, just makes me more certain that the persecution I face, the plot of which I am a victim, is inescapable as long as I am in this nation – and it will continue even if I return to the Continent. I thought that crossing the sea might free me from my enemies' grasp, but I was wrong. Perhaps a more remote island would be better, perhaps the sun and warmth of Corsica would alleviate the complaints that are unbearable in these conditions. Corsica, where I would be treated with respect, where I could live in honest independence and be consulted from time to time on important matters of constitutional procedure, where my thinking would be recognised as having merit and genuine worth – but no, it is not the right place for me; too barren, too rocky, I would be too involved in the day-to-day activities of people – I want to be alone, with the plants, not giving advice to a young government trying to secure its place in the world. They would ask me to speak in public, to publish, and I hope to do neither of those things again.

Slow, weary progress. A growing sense of reluctance and futility. The motivations which first inspired my work have evaporated and now I find it a great ordeal to set pen to paper. I would rather be asleep, but apparently that is impossible for me now. Through Davenport I have sold most of my books, and anyway my eyesight is so poor now that I cannot read much at all. I cannot play music at night, on the tired and creaking spinet here, for fear of disturbing the house, further alienating the servants; so I sit and stare at my work, the stacks of paper covered in shameful words, and I try to build up the courage to read them back, or to set more words down, but I fail myself, and I remain sitting where I am, paralysed for hours, feeling stupid and wasteful, until the first notes of birdsong come into the room, and I am sent back to the days reading with my father, the lark's song calls me to bed, in the hopes of gleaning some fractious hours of rest; but I don't feel the joy I felt in my early years now, just the melancholy pain of my isolation and illness.

Once, I was capable of thought, at least to some extent. I have philosophised, discoursed, reasoned, proven, disputed, argued, claimed, demonstrated, conceptualised, and so on – I have developed systems, critiqued systems, articulated rebuttals and responses; I've done it all. All that is gone now: I don't have any more use for it, I don't want any more abstractions, no, nothing more like that, I couldn't do them if I wanted to, I am no longer a philosopher, and God willing, soon, I will no longer be a writer of any kind either – once this account of myself and my life is done, I will stop for good – I will stop receiving letters from the few correspondents who still communicate with me in my exile, I will never again spoil paper with my words – perhaps I might still copy out a little music from time to time, when I need to earn my bread, but I will put no more thoughts on the page; soon I will be as stupid and unencumbered by writing as a dog. How happy Sultan is in comparison with me. So now that I have put all that behind me, or will soon have done so, it is extremely inconvenient that even here in my remoteness from the world I am recognised as something which I no longer am. I have no opinions, read nothing, I hear nothing, I think nothing. Plants are my sole focus, and even in that field I fail to remember anything more than the most basic and rudimentary bits of information. Boothby asked me the other day if I had read some book or other, or if I had any thoughts on something the government here had been doing, something to do with unrest over the price of bread. How could I? I know better by now to develop any opinions on matters of state, particularly opinions about a state which has granted me asylum – uncertain and tortured as my status here is. No, I told him: If we are to be friends, you must forget that you have ever read a single word of mine, forget that I ever wrote or published anything, associate with me purely for the delight which you take in my company. The rest is nonsense, an encumbrance, a barrier to true friendship. The friends I seek must see me for who I am: as a man unburdened by learning or reason, but free, simple, honest, earnest, open. I dream among the plants, wandering about the countryside absent-mindedly. Politics, the role of the state, society, government, none of these words mean anything to me any more, nor will they ever again.

I sit down to write. The sentences I had composed in full during my walks among the moors have evaporated. The paper in front of me, the wind howling outside. My mind a waste. I read back the last pages I had written and felt sick. The usual pains. My head feels numb. I think about going back to bed. The room is poorly illuminated. The window reveals a thick grey mass of cloud above the flat, brown, empty fields. There is no way to tell what time it is from the light outside, no intimation of whether it is morning or afternoon. I feel as if I were sat in a purgatorial void, condemned to try to justify myself through words which would not come. In bed the night before, I had thought things through so thoroughly, so completely, that I had expected sitting down today would be a liberation. But instead I find myself sinking again into gloom. My pains are not yet bad enough today for me to give up. It is too cold to walk. Thérèse is shut in her rooms. It is important that I write. I need to write my confessions. It is imperative. My head in my hands. Eventually, after some time in this attitude of despondency, an image floats up before me. I saw Vercellis. Madame de Vercellis, a severe, cold, aloof, mean-spirited woman. I was her footman. We were in Turin. She lay in bed, dying from the cancer in her breast, her strictness gone, replaced with a strange morbid gaiety, joking and laughing with the servants, with whom before she had always been so hard and unmoving. The smell of death was settling around her. Everyone was assembled, a convivial atmosphere half-masking the approaching event. The other servants, lackeys, attendants, hangers-on, family schemers hoping for a payment which would soon fall to them, all gathered around the deathbed. She gave no signs of her pain, refused to groan or to complain, or to cry out. Her death was in her, aggressive and painful, and she sought to conquer it through humour, through light spirits, talking to everyone, even those she had scorned in her health. I was surprised; impressed. The approach of death transformed her, the prospect of Heaven. She became a good-humoured person, unfamiliar and strange to me. Perhaps this was how she had acted as a girl. Eventually, after two days had passed like this, she grew quiet. The end was drawing near, the bitterness had taken root, it was clear to everyone in the room, it was inescapable now. Between jokes she started to look a little frightened, though she took pains to hide this. The last words came, the last breaths, the last glances, she stopped speaking, and started, quietly, to whine a little, to groan, nothing too ostentatious or mournful, just a grunt of discomfort, the whimper of a scared creature, a few tears came to her eyes, it was finally the end, a devout atmosphere descended and took hold of us, we waited, sombre, quiet, a portentous moment, her joking of the past two days gone, silence fell on the room. We stood around her. She lay on her side. Her eyes closed lightly, but her chest still moved, very gently. Suddenly, she broke the silence herself. Madame de Vercellis, that severe and rigorously intellectual woman, in her very last moments emitted an enormous and lengthy fart. It is perhaps not uncommon, but it struck me enormously. "Good," she said, rolling onto her back and staring blankly at the ceiling. "Good. A woman who can fart is not dead." Nobody replied. A few servants looked at each other. Her eyes closed, for the last time. Soon after, I was dismissed and left the house and Turin for good.

All day today I felt as if somebody were missing, as

though they had just stepped out of the room and would return at any moment. I spent the afternoon with Davenport and his grandchildren, who were learning arithmetic – with great pleasure I joined in the lesson and found I was able to solve a very large sum entirely in my head. My faculties are not going entirely, then. The children are a comfort and a source of joy, to me as much as to Davenport – they are orphans, and my friend has suggested that they might be further educated according to my own principles – a very flattering suggestion, and of course one which I think could be very sensible. But Davenport is a doting and perhaps overindulgent grandfather, and it is impossible for me to gauge fully whether he has understood my writing on the subject properly, or whether, like so many others, he has misread me; perhaps anyway it is too late for the children to begin according to my schema; but I cannot air these misgivings in person, I merely try to nudge things along. But who was it I felt to be absent? It was a strange sensation, which followed me even when I stepped out alone for a walk around the terraces, that at any moment I might turn and make a remark to my companion, as soon as they had returned from whatever it was they were doing, or had caught up with me. Occasionally I was struck by the desire to explain something gently and simply, as if to a child. I found myself describing what I saw under my breath. I did not interrupt the lessons of Davenport's wards to take them botanising; perhaps I felt as if a child of my own should have been there with me. But that thought is too painful, and I must recoil from it, I can't allow myself to dwell on that particular wound, not in the condition I find myself in these days. Where are they now? I am sure we did the best for them – I could never have wanted to expose them to the life of vagrancy I have been forced into; we made our choice, more than once, according to both custom and necessity. But I feel the lack of their company, their trust. Perhaps their presence would help Thérèse, who is lost here. Perhaps I would have written less, caused less scandal, if I had been busy with our children alongside my musical copying – needing to provide for them would have given me less time for the things which have brought me so much suffering. But no, how could I have provided? – I already had to support Thérèse's family, her mother, they relied on me, we would have been too many, the Hospital will have saved my children from the treachery of the educated classes and will have given them an opportunity to be happy, honest, natural, in the way that I was as a boy, before all of this. Still, when I look in the sweet and trusting faces of Phoebe and Davis, something tears at my heart, and I must look away before too long.

The memory of the death of Mme de Vercellis is tender for a moment; I am filled with a kind of respectful amusement, proud to have been in her service despite how unfriendly she had seemed to me before her final days, and despite how much I would now chafe at the servitude I was forced into during my youth. But soon this feeling starts to be less secure, as if something lay underneath it which I have long ignored, something more serious and shameful, which I have deliberately hidden from myself, an experience which I cannot confront fully or allow myself to remember, but which nevertheless feels insistent and important. I cringe at my writing, here in the cave, as it comes back to me in full. One of the most shameful events of my life, about which it is excruciating for me to think. If only I could return to that time and take a different course of action, I might now be happy, I might not be in the predicament I find myself in. But what happened more than thirty years ago cannot be undone now through my feeling of guilt, it cannot be expiated, and all I can hope to do is to lay bare my remorse and admit to my grievously poor behaviour, the cowardice with which I sought to escape my fate, the injustice with which I acted. Mme de Vercellis was dead. The house was in disarray, trying to find a new equilibrium. Much was uncertain. Of course, in such periods, it is inevitable that things go missing. The establishment was breaking up and an inventory was taken. Found to be missing was a pink and silver ribbon, quite old, which belonged to Mlle Pontal, the niece of the wife of Lorenzi – the head of service in the household. Mlle Pontal was a sly woman who had served as Mme de Vercellis' maid, and who had stopped me from visiting her bedside while her will was being written. I saw the ribbon, I wanted it, I took it. I could have stolen something else which was worth much more; this ribbon was worthless, but it pleased me to look at it. It was found among my things, quite easily, because after I stole it I realised it was the act of stealing which appealed to me more than the ribbon itself, which, now that it was mine, was no longer of any interest to me. It was found in a pocket. I was questioned. I should say now that I feel no shame over this pathetic petty thieving. It is how I behaved under interrogation which makes me flush, which makes me hang my head and feel sick from the shame. I was questioned by Lorenzi himself, my enemy, one of the first conspirators against me, who unknowingly then established the pattern which has dogged me my entire life, who gave me my first foretaste of the degradation of being a victim of the malicious play of intrigue from which I am unable to escape. Under his questioning I simply, and quite easily at first, lied. I blushed and said Marion had stolen the ribbon. Marion! The beautiful, fresh-complexioned kitchen girl, sweet, modest, unimpeachable, sensible, trustworthy. How they could have believed my accusation baffles me still, but they at least had to follow it up. They summoned her, and I grew bolder as the situation grew more humiliating; I accused her to her face. Her soft and clear eyes. She remained silent and looked me with pity, without a hint of pleading. Yes, I denounced her again, and once more. She had stolen the ribbon, and given it to me. It seems ridiculous that they could believe such an outright falsehood. But then, how could she defend herself? It is after years of being the victim of unjust persecution that I can now understand the fear and horror that she must have felt, the shame, at being accused falsely of a crime and being unable to defend herself by no other means than merely repeating her innocence – the cruel experience of the innocent stammering in front of their slick and trenchant accuser, in a situation they do not understand; it rends my heart to think of it. The anger she must have felt towards me! But she didn't express it – she denied any involvement in the theft again, and again, and turned to me and said: You make me very sad, but I should not like to be in your place. How wise and beautiful she was then. What a monster I was! To our judges it must have appeared to be a conflict between an impetuous and stubborn devil and a calm and serene angel. In the end we were both dismissed, with the sentiment expressed that the guilty one's conscience would avenge the innocent. What happened to Marion after this incident? How could she hope to obtain another position with this mark against her name? Why had I been so obstinate in my lies, in my betrayal? I have tried to forget this incident but find myself haunted by my behaviour then; it comes back to me, this miserable scene, when I lie awake at night. I have seen Marion approaching my bedside at night, as if to reproach me for my heartless calumny. My life has since been stormy, and this early falsehood of mine has deprived me even of the certainty of innocence, and the sweet consolation which that certainty provides in the face of persecution. Perhaps I feel as if I were the cause of my own misfortune, my subsequent trials have been the result of this one act, which shames me still. I have never spoken of it to any one, not even Maman. I must admit to it in full honesty now, without trying to mitigate the seriousness of my misdeed. Remorse sleeps while fate is kind, but it grows sharp in adversity. For a long time I managed to bury this incident, but whenever my fortunes have taken a turn for the worse it has returned to me, repeating itself in my darkest moments and longest nights. I had perhaps hoped to give the ribbon to Marion, and I responded to being discovered in my theft by trying to avoid disgrace or shame; I was not worried about punishment, but humiliation was the worst fate I could imagine. Little did I suspect then that this act would leave an indelible wound of disgrace and shame on my heart and that even now, decades later and in a foreign country, I am visited by the stern and pitiful look of reproach on Marion's face. And perhaps I have benefitted even from this – the telling of this one lie has led to my lifelong horror of untruth, and it has encouraged me to avoid any further misdeed which might be considered truly reprehensible or even criminal. I have atoned for this sin by the persecutions I have faced since, and continue to face. Marion has been avenged, though she could never know it.

In the woods earlier, two of David's silent emissaries

were busying themselves with the pretence of collecting some scraps of wood, taking it home from the forests to keep warm. As if they couldn't buy wood to burn with the pay they receive from their master. I suppose being employed to keep watch on a prisoner as regular in his habits as I am is not very lucrative. I walk the same paths every day, botanise at the same spots, look at the same plants, each time as if it were the first. On some days I see my guards, on others they manage to conceal themselves more effectively. It's rarely the same person they send, sometimes it is a child, or someone dressed in the garb of one of the lead miners, blackened with dirt from below the ground, sometimes an old man with tattered clothing collecting things from the forests and scraps from the last patches of wasteland. All are disguised, but I'm sure they send their reports when I'm out of their sight once more, those that can write will do so, sending a letter to David directly, the others presumably dictate or deliver an oral report to a supervisor in the village. It makes me laugh, really: an extraordinary amount of effort, time and expense to keep watch on an ageing and harmless person like myself, who does nothing and poses no threat to anyone, who seeks only obscurity and some time with the plants. They can't get anything from me now, since they already have so much; let them watch me. The net tightens around me, but I take care to show them that it does not bother me. But what can I hope for, when all is done? I will see no end to my persecutions – no chance of a quiet withdrawal from the world – I will spend the rest of my time on this earth hunted and monitored, surveilled by an authority which never shows its true nature, but which assumes the form of my friends and reveals them to be its emissaries. What is it that I did to earn the scorn of this authority, so that they pursue me even here, so that they do not allow me the independence and freedom I have spent so long trying to find; what sin have I committed, beyond expressing the contents of my heart openly and freely, looking humanity in the face and saying: This is who I am and what I think. I don't go as far as others, who seek to tear down the whole edifice of society – I seek only to reveal the missteps the world has taken, but I believe that however bad things are now, they could indeed be much worse. For this, they stone my house, they burn my books, they make and burn effigies of me, they hound me, eject me from cities, issue arrest warrants, spill copious amounts of ink rebutting what I have written, lure me to a country where I have no friends, place me constantly under guard, with the complaisance of those who once swore they loved me. I am the victim of a great and monstrous plot, and I see no possibilities open to me, no chance of extricating myself from it; no, nothing, no hope, nothing, no.

I have spent much time with Granville and Mary at Calwick recently, grateful to be taken out of myself by them while the weather has remained so pleasant over the past few weeks. Granville is considering adapting his gardens, making improvements to them, and he seeks my advice, which I give under a pretence of not wanting to presume too much. But I am full of ideas for what could be achieved there; his grounds could truly become blissful. I go alone and spend long hours there, striding back over the fields in the late dying rays of the sun. Thérèse is angry with me; she says she is sick of England, but in truth she is jealous of Mary, who I have been perhaps overly attentive towards. Ah, Mary: she is young, attentive; she is sweet to me, humours me. I become foolish around her, but I cannot help myself. Of course Thérèse resents appearing as merely my housekeeper, my gouvernante – but I promised her I would never marry her, and she has accepted this so far. Hence our decision about the children – saving them from the shame of illegitimacy and freeing them from the accident of me being their father. To revenge herself, Thérèse has been telling me at length about the night she spent in transit to England from Paris in the company of young Boswell, delayed in their crossing for a week. I try not to listen to her, but her stories of disloyalty do something to me that I can't explain; they hurt and thrill me at the same time – she knows my desires well enough and knows how to humiliate me for them. She tells her story in a way that casts her in an honourable light, him in a clownish one, but they imply that more happened in reality than she will admit to me; she just talks of one night in Dover, just after their crossing: Boswell has drunk a bottle of wine and is toiling and grunting away on top of her, she feels nothing and tells him he should learn to use his hands – a charming vignette – yes, she wants to undermine me, and him, and every one that isn't her. Boswell wrote to me recently, in fact, his letter was accompanied by a volume he had written about a trip to Corsica taken, apparently, inspired by me. I did not read the book and replied only to tell him he might consider having himself bled once in a while.

Last night a frantic evening and night spent writing, almost desperately; my old problems in compositions left me and I sat for hours, covering pages with a productivity unlike anything I am used to. I don't know if it is well-written, but it came from the heart, propelled by a feeling of urgent desperation, so even if it is stylistically reprehensible, it will at least be honest. The need to account for myself, to justify my existence and my behaviour – not to excuse it but to lay it bare in all of its failings – this is what must have spurred me on – the desire to prove my enemies wrong, to reveal myself to be more wretched than they suspect me to be, to mount a defence and show them that no matter how harshly they judge me, they cannot approach the standards against which I judge myself. I see my last hours approaching; I start to think that I have lived too long already, and so the urgency of my task is increasingly imperative.

Mary has sent me a collar for Sultan, one she made herself. A lovely object, which I could not resist myself. I took it from its wrapping and reverently set it around my own neck, imagining myself at her mercy. I blush to the roots of my hair. A stirring – the old desires back again, dormant until now. I don't want to get carried away, and my condition prevents me from following my fantasies too far, but something in the collar speaks to that part of myself I have always struggled to express, which has always remained unarticulated out of shame, or fear of being laughed at, or disappointed – my desire to be beaten, punished by a beautiful woman. I cannot reveal this to Mary, and I suspect I'll never talk of it to anyone, but I have been dwelling on it again recently, revisiting the sweet memory of my first punishments at the hands of Mlle Lambercier when I was eight years old – that mixture of sensuality which was half shame, half pleasure, sweetly painful. To fall on my knees before a masterful mistress, to obey her commands, to have to beg for her forgiveness! I wrote to Mary to thank her for the collar, telling her that it aroused my jealousy and that I have deprived Sultan of the pleasure of being its first wearer. Perhaps too forward of me, and I might reveal too much, but I have never yet managed to express these desires, and feel that they must be so deeply secret that I could not reveal them even accidentally. They have never been realised, they will not be realised now – I would throw myself to my knees in front of Mary and beg her to bind me in chains and to humiliate me, but I will never tell her that, and I can see no harm in a little flirtation, despite the rage I see building in Thérèse.

Last night I began to write about exposing myself to women as a young man, hiding in dark corners with my trousers around my ankles, the cold stone against my skin, the labyrinth of cellars next to a well, women coming and going to collect water, the dampness, shaking with anticipation and fear, torn between wanting to be caught and punished and wanting to escape – the large man with the moustache who chased and threatened me – gratitude to him for letting me get away unharmed. Humiliation. It all came over me, the torpor that descended upon me afterwards; the mindless compulsion preceding the act – as if something had taken possession of my body, and I could do nothing until I had fulfilled its command. I longed to be beaten but I couldn't ask a soul – I was shy, embarrassed, ashamed; I have never been able to ask for what I really want, even with Thérèse, who takes the initiative herself to get from me what pleasures she can – not much these days, a cursory stiffness which causes me pain, and then a reluctant trickle of sperm. Revisiting the old fantasies, how recklessly I acted, stirred something inside me, perhaps evoked by the feeling I got from wearing Sultan's collar from Mary – if only I could ask her to deliver on the promise which that collar suggests to me. I thought I would become free from these fantasies, but they only fade to a murmur for a few weeks at a time, before returning with a full and resounding insistency when I think they have disappeared for good.

Vomiting: I ate some berries from a tree which I obviously should have left alone. Small, purplish, round. They were bitter but I still merrily chewed a handful as I walked. I don't remember where the tree was, but I was sick over the side of a small bridge and was forced to return home. My stomach is still knotted and cramped tight, but I hope the poison has been expelled. A stupid mistake; I should be more careful with what I eat on my walks – I have been plucking berries and leaves without thinking. The animals know what to avoid instinctively; what a shame it is that we have been civilised out of that capability.

Another long walk today, out all afternoon, into the evening. The old oscillations again: the intense energy I had previously managed to bring to my writing has left me; now when I sit down to write in my cave I feel a mix of disgust for the work, shame for my past misdeeds, and a deep melancholy for the loss of the happy days of my childhood. Writing has only ever brought me unhappiness. I should have stuck to music, or I should have stayed longer in my apprenticeship – the watchmaking of Geneva, or the engraving that once so enamoured me. Among the delicate tools of my father, the hammers, the pliers, the lathes, the oiling sticks, the medallions I engraved for myself in secret. Now I have no skill for the use of tools, my eyes are too bad for the delicate work needed in those trades that I was half-trained in. Instead, I am sure that the thing which would give me the most happiness, something which could please me until my final hours, would be the discovery of a single new plant. It wouldn't have to be particularly beautiful, or very useful, or even interesting to anyone else – merely unknown or undocumented. I dream of it. This would please me more than any prize from any Academy, or a new edition of my works, one which would remain in print until the last days of mankind and find its true readers in the distant future. All my writing is for nothing, I should have abandoned it long ago. It has brought me nothing but displeasure and persecution. I long for obscurity – here I am away from the world but the newspapers still fill their pages with gossip about me and my time in London and Paris, reports from hangers-on and hack journalists; the mood has shifted even further from its high pitch of triumphant adulation to new lows of fickle scorning and malignancy. I thought the people in this country might love me, but they are now fully turned against me. For what purpose? What do they hope to gain by mocking me like this? I have nothing for them. I write my confessions so I no longer have any score to settle with the world, I have made my peace with God, I will no longer be accused of anything which I have not admitted myself. When I finish the work then perhaps I will be allowed to die. I don't care what happens to me after they're complete, only that I will have displayed myself as I was, as I am. But it's hard going at the moment, and I find it easier to walk out in the fields alone, or with Sultan. The weather is bad again. The rain comes across the sky in sheets and the wind howls incessantly. I feel for the sheep out there on the barren peatland. I envy the rabbits snug in their warren. The summer has drawn to an end, if it can be called a summer. The nights feel unending again. I saw some early mushrooms, red on the outside but yellow where they had been gnawed at by an animal, blackish in places. I don't know what it was. I should try to learn the names of the fungi here too, I suppose. I once had some of that knowledge, but it's long gone, slipped from my grasp. I don't care about eating them; I don't want them for nourishment. It's enough for me to just know the names of things, to know where they live, what conditions they like. Then, when I see something I can recognise, I can call it by its name, and it is like being met by a friend you don't expect to see. Except plants ask nothing of you. The ferns here are remarkable – the bracken and gorse up on the hills – the mosses, the herbs, the oaks. This country could be like paradise if the weather were less dismal.

*

TIME PASSES. Over the fields, climbing the new-built stone walls, the recent boundaries, the forests being slowly cleared to make room for the sheep, the smell of peat being burnt, moors being ravaged, the sound of grouse being disturbed from their resting places in the dark gloom under the browning and decaying bracken, the ground in the woods scattered with a layer of cob nuts, fungi erupting at the base of a dead tree trunk, the berries black and starting to wither on the bramble, the season turns and the weather fades with it, days begin with fog or mist, drizzle occasionally gives way to the last few hours of warmth from the sun that there will be for months, the labourers are out for the harvest, they collect dead wood from the forests, laying in a store for the winter, around the corner; leaves brown, red, orange, gold, black, horse chestnuts on the ground, long warm slanting rays of light over the crops, an adolescent fox walking alone at dusk, the still hare stopped in a field, near a thistle, eyes and ears twitching, more robins in the holly, which already has its first red berries.

Mid-September now, just after the harvest moon, a dark ridge of cloud, but no rain; one or two orange leaves drift past the window, briefly illuminated in a thin ray of sunlight. The horse chestnuts are out. I am told by Mr Walton that this year has seen a particularly poor harvest. In the village the men stand around in idle groups, with drawn and closed faces, looking hungry. The price of food has increased substantially;

I notice it too, and the labourers can't afford very much to eat. Many of the larger towns have seen unrest, mobs of starved workers caused disorder – at least, that's how it is described in the newspapers. I do what I can to help those that I see here; I press some change into a hand here and there, I help as many as I can, so does Thérèse, but I know my actions don't resolve anything. They need cheaper food, not more money. I have been hungry myself, in my younger years, and am lucky not to be so now. In my youth I walked for days with only some hard bread and cheese to sustain me. Ah, but I was young then. I was free, unfettered, alone in the world, and young. Not broken down by the hard work to which these men are forced. These men are free too, in a sense: free from all possessions other than their own bodies, which become worth less and less on the market the longer the food shortages last. The winter will be difficult. I don't know much about the situation, other than the little I read and what I see for myself, a few remarks here and there; all quite vague. I have experienced the displeasure of mobs at first hand. It is in my interest to be generous to the villagers, and I would help – even if pity, and the hatred I feel for a world which allows some to move between multiple houses and eat until they suffer from gout while others starve to death in unheated rooms – didn't move me to be kind already.

I am in the hospice for converts in Turin. How old am I? Before Vercellis – sixteen or seventeen. Geneva is behind me forever, or so I think at the time; I have seen the last of my master, the apprenticeship abandoned, the tools set down for good – I had already spent some time drifting around the Savoy quite aimlessly, stopping outside the gates of large houses in the hopes of some adventure or romance, my head already full of the daydreams which will take up so much of my life. I have squandered the little hoard of money I had acquired and am forced into the arms of the Catholic Church, which will secure me a position and tend to my soul, settling both my spiritual and financial crises at once. Through my conversion I have been introduced to Mme de Warens, Maman, but I cannot write about her yet – there is too much to say and my thoughts are disordered – focus now on Turin. Among the priests in the hospice disputing Augustine, Gregory, Ambrose, Ignatius, Tertullian, Cyril, Jerome, the other church fathers, I could handle them all easily, discourse on them nimbly, precocious as I was; I held my ground against the sophistry of the teaching brothers, though I quickly grew tired of argument and was always in the end overcome. Did I believe in what I was doing there? It is hard to say now, from this distance. Perhaps, certainly to some degree, but I also knew that I would be clothed and fed and have somewhere to sleep for a while, before I had to make any more decisions. It was a rest. The other converts seemed to be in more or less the same situation – undesirable companions who instinctively I felt were below me in rank and station – but who was I? A runaway apprentice from Geneva, with a small amount of disordered book learning that I had grasped where I could – though that was still better than the other characters who had taken refuge in the bosom of the church. One night I had a very strange experience, which I have tried not to examine too closely, or think about for too long, because of the complex parcel of disgust, shame, and excitement it provokes in me. Two of the other converts were Croatian, I believe, but they tried to pass themselves off more ambiguously or exotically, claiming to have spent their lives wandering around Europe, freed from conscience, doing as they pleased and converting to whichever religion would offer them a bed for the night and a few coins when it suited them, and then passing on without a second thought, sinning wherever they went. They would tell me lengthy stories about their experiences in their own jargon, and I would listen, rapt and horrified. The evening I am thinking of took place a few weeks after my arrival. One of these characters had apparently taken a shine to me. He had been trying to perform small favours for me, doing little services, sharing his food from his plate; he would spend his spare time trying to talk to me, though his language was erratic and sometimes incomprehensible; sometimes he would gaze at me at length, in silence, a slight smile on his lips – not unlike the look that was fixed upon me that night by the good David. I did nothing much to repulse my admirer, perhaps naively, I simply thought that he was affectionate towards me out of friendship, motivated by some opaque reason. He grew gradually more familiar towards me, getting closer to me all the time. We slept in the same room. On the night I am thinking of, things came to a head, and he suggested to me that we might share a bed – it was cold, he said, we would be warmer together – it was cold, certainly, but I said that my bed would be too narrow for two; he suggested his, but it was no wider than my own, and I refused again. I remember his smell clearly, tobacco, sweat, filth. He did not bathe often. I felt that I had to refuse this request, I was right to do so, but I didn't do so with complete conviction – I was not too adamant. I suppose I was pleased to be an object of desire – I didn't want this admirer, but of course my fantasies all had an erotic and sensuous element at that time, even if my idea of what sexuality meant was childish and based only on imagination. While wandering Savoy I had masturbated outside walled gardens, thinking of the wealthy and beautiful women who would discover me and punish me; I had masturbated among the ferns in the forests, pricked myself with brambles, longing to be discovered and punished in the discovery, quivering with fright as I ejaculated onto the tree trunk against which I braced myself. But nobody else had given me any bodily pleasure since the inadvertent thrill of my childhood punishments, and I hadn't yet touched another body – here was somebody clearly willing, although he was more than a little repugnant to me. I did not necessarily want to rebuff him too sharply, in case he withdrew his affections entirely. Perhaps this was cowardice. It is a complicated position to be in, but one which is perhaps familiar to many. After I refused to share a bed with him he left me alone for some time, but in the early morning, between matins and lauds, we found ourselves alone in the assembly hall, whether by chance or by his contrivance I don't know. He resumed his caresses, holding me close to him and kissing me on the cheek and the neck, his hands starting to roam over my body. His smell filled my nostrils. I was torn between an inchoate desire and a feeling of repulsion. I tried to refuse him, to push him away, but he clung to me, growing increasingly insistent, his hands began to caress below my waist, soon he was rubbing and stroking me, but I tried to remain still, feeling a sweet pain, my stomach starts to shrink and become heavy, nauseous, his breathing quickens in my eye, my own breath quickens, he moves his free hand to mine and begins to guide it, but I try to resist, I don't want to give him any pleasure other than that which he can get from desiring me and hoping to have me, I don't want to touch him but I can feel his warmth against me, his hardness, my hand is around him, his hands on my waist and my cock, he is heaving and toiling away at me, but too roughly, the glimpse of pleasure I sensed is gone as quickly as it arrived and it is as if I wake up from a dream, I see the position I am in and I recoil, I push back against him, disentangle myself, cry out, I don't want it, I free my hand from him, stiffen it so he can't manipulate it anymore, I step back and at the same time I feel the warm wetness on my palm, and see a creamy mess dripping onto the floor from my hand. His eyes half-closed, he turns and leaves me. I am shaken. I run to the balcony and breathe as deeply as I can, huge breaths, regular, trying to calm myself. Eventually I became still and my mind became cloudy. I did not understand what had happened to me and felt incredibly confused, at a loss. My body felt sore, tired. I didn't know what to do; I was nauseous and felt a tightness in my chest, near my heart, a feeling of anxiety in the pit of my stomach. I was confounded. Almost immediately after this experience I felt an urge I can't quite explain: I had to talk about what had happened to anyone who would listen, to try to explain it, to air it, to display the shame – such that it might not fester and ferment in my mind, and might become clear somehow. But my openness about the event just led to my being rebuked by one of the principals of the hospice, who quite freely and openly told me that I should feel no affront, I should see that being the object of desire was no sin, that what had happened was only a mild case of fornication – immoral, yes, but not so serious as all that. To the principal, and the ecclesiastic who listened in to our conversation, licking his lips in the corner of the room, the event seemed normal, I need not make a fuss over a trifle such as this, and anyway it can't have been as bad as all that, perhaps I enjoyed it a little even. My suitor did not speak to me again after the event, and a week later he was baptised, entered into the church –

until he converted again to some other faith – and with great ceremony left the hospice. I never saw him again.

My recollections of the encounter in Turin led me on to other similar experiences, ones from which I have similarly shrunk in recollection. I cannot exactly remember when they happened, or the order in which they happened. One when I must have been about twenty. I was on a journey to Lyon, sitting in the Bellecour alone, after a poor supper, ruminating on my miserable situation. A man in a cap came and sat beside me – he was dressed in the costume of one of the silk weavers of that city, his days spent among the looms or the mulberry bushes and the worms. I can hardly remember his face, but I can clearly remember his cap and his clothing. He started a conversation with me in a bland and cool manner. I replied. We talked about everyday things, nothing memorable, exactly the kind of conversation you might have with a stranger on some empty evening. We talked quite normally like this for about ten minutes or so, then he looked at me, and without changing the tone of his voice or his attitude whatsoever he suggested that we have some fun together. I didn't understand him, and waited for him to suggest something more concrete, but instead of speaking further, he simply took out his penis and started to stroke it. I tried to look ahead and ignore him, unsure of what was happening; he was sitting right up against me, though we were not quite touching, he seemed to not be interested in my body, but I could see him harden out of the corner of my eye. I tried not to acknowledge it, but found myself frozen, eventually I couldn't help but glance down at his tumescence; seeing this he was encouraged and suggested that I had my own fun while he had his, we didn't have to touch each other at all, just the thing for a lonely night, a bit of company. Around that time my addiction to masturbation was relentless; I was constantly sneaking away to let my fantasies play out. It would have been easy to do it there, in his company, and I looked at him again, and felt a stirring of my own. But I felt uncomfortable, soon the repulsion overtook me again and I stood up and walked quickly away; he didn't call after me, he didn't seem to feel rejected, he had suggested it so naturally that it seemed impossible for me to accept his offer. Did I want to? I don't know, but I avoided having to confront the possibility, and I ran away. As I left him my head span, and I ended up down by the river, having taken the opposite route to where my lodgings lay. I looked down into the murky water and found myself full of the old feeling of shame, confusion, loneliness.

Those days which followed, with Mme de Warens, Maman, were the closest I had been to a sense of security for some time, and perhaps the last time in my life I felt anything like belonging. Yes, she was my friend, but she was more, she was like my mother, a confidant, eventually my lover – she gave me my first complete sexual encounters, and I responded to them by feeling as if I had committed incest – sobbing as I made my boyish movements on top of her, while she lay calm and passive, gently stroking my hair. Those days were happy; I knew that eventually I would find the success I knew was due to me, but I was in no rush to go out and seek it, I was settled and idle, I did as I pleased without any thought of actively making something of myself, I was loved and I loved in turn. But here I also tasted the first real bitterness found in the disappointment that comes from getting something you think you want, finally possessing an object you have dreamt of and longed for. I had fantasised about her and about others so often that the first time Maman and I slept together there was no possible hope of it comparing favourably with my dreams – especially because I was still too shy to ask her to perform the acts for which I really longed. I had to be led by her entirely, since I was shy and stupid, and the sadness which followed was hard to bear, the depressing and shameful fact of it all. I had some pleasure, of course, but I was unwell at the time, and my body seemed to me even then to be only a source of disgust and horror, deeply unpleasant. Since then, all of my erotic encounters have been of the same kind: the pleasures of the flesh have never come close to living up to their ideal state, and yet they continue to take up so much of my inner life – I cannot free myself from the fantasies to which I have been addicted since I was a child. But in thinking over my time with Maman, I feel as if I were back there in Annecy and Chambéry. I think of the other people in her life, the men with whom she surrounded herself. When I arrived at her house there was already Anet. Eventually I took precedence in Maman's affections, as Anet grew older, less handsome, less appealing, more bogged down in the day-to-day details of life in the service of Mme de Warens, less like a pet, more like an employee. I displaced Anet. He was a peasant from Moutru, who knew how to gather the correct herbs for a medicinal tisane which Maman claimed to need. He was slow, deliberate in his movements and speech, laconic, occasionally sententious; he could also be irascible and impetuous at times. He died from pleurisy, out collecting génépi one day in the mountains. By that time Maman had stopped sleeping with him and had taken to spending part of her nights in my rooms, in my sickbed. Anet had met this change in his fortunes with a stoic blankness, apparently apathetic to his demotion in Maman's eyes. Presumably Anet had himself displaced someone when he arrived, before I in turn displaced him. I respected Anet. It had been Anet who first tried to introduce me to botany, but his was a practical approach, one which saw the plants only for their use in an apothecary; an approach that at the time I associated with quack druggists. I scorned botany at first, even though it is now clear to me that it is the one activity suited to my personality, the only one which allows my natural inclinations and demeanour to shine forth. When the time came for my eventual replacement by Mme de Warens, spurred on by my inability to recognise what rare thing I had in fact attained in Maman's house, motivated by a vain desire to wander off and see something of the world, I wished that I had been able to emulate his philosophical calmness at being ousted by a younger man. I was not detached in the way that Anet was. I came back to Maman after some time away in the nearby towns, spent pretending to be a musician, and I found myself replaced by a journeyman wigmaker called Wintzenreid, a vain and stupid snob who pretended that he was descended from some obscure branch of the nobility. When I returned to the house, Les Charmettes, and found myself confronted by this loud and vapid moron, it was as if the earth slipped into a deep and impenetrable shadow; I saw my dreams of a happy future vanish, and I was left with the unappetising prospect of a bland and savourless life ahead of me. It was as though I had been half-killed there and then. Anet had taught me some things. I thought that perhaps, if nothing else, I might be able to pass on these small bits of wisdom to Wintzenreid in my turn. But he only saw me as a tiresome pedant who used tedious lectures to obstruct his path to the erotic dalliances with Maman, who now became very cold towards me, would barely speak to me, all the while remaining full of effusive adoration for Wintzenreid, whom she made me call brother. Brother! Maman's new lover was to be my brother. The feeling of having committed incest, which had come over me after our first night together, returned. From that point on I gave up all sexual aspirations regarding Maman and saw her only through the eyes of a son. Wintzenreid was an abominable man, one who, not content with his capturing Maman, kept an elderly red-headed chambermaid in his service, without a single tooth in her mouth, who provided him with services which I recoil from describing, to which Maman turned a blind eye. I became isolated and aloof and began to be aware that I was perhaps no longer at home in Maman's company, her house was no longer as open to me as it once was, and I would perhaps soon have to find my own path forward, away from her and her care.

A crisp and bright autumn morning, the full moon still visible in the sky, wavering above the trees. I feel for the first time in weeks a kind of optimism, a sense that the mental contortions I had been going through recently were determined more by the weather than by anything else, that on days like this, when I could do as I pleased, when I could be out in the woods all day, wandering and collecting my specimens, it was as if I might in fact be approaching something like happiness; that it was only during the dark and morose days, when the clouds hung low over the fields and the world felt cold and empty that my mind wandered and started to pick away at the various ways I felt myself to have been wronged. How weak this makes me feel, though, that time spent outdoors, in the light, in the clearness of the sky, in fine weather, could alter my mood so profoundly. As I walk through the woods, looking closely at the moulds which flourish in this season, the puffballs swollen and on the point of bursting open, the bracket fungi on the tree trunks, I can feel the tension and disappointment of the last few weeks sloughing off me. I saw an enormous yellow mushroom, growing on the trunk of a tree, being harvested by a local woman, poorly dressed. She looked shy when I approached but carried on with her task despite my observation. She collected a basketful, but there was still a lot left on the trunk. After she left I examined it myself; it was spongy, with a very faint smell of apricot. A joy, of a very specific kind, which I will cherish. The autumn so far had been wet, misty, cold and claustrophobic; my body had suffered and I could only look ahead to the coming months in a mood of deep despair and growing dread; alone, unwell, stuck indoors with the ambient hostility of the household and Thérèse's ever-growing irritation – this is not a prospect which appealed to me. But I feel that a day like this might lift my spirits sufficiently for a week or so, that as long as I might have occasional opportunities to take myself out of myself, to examine the gradual progression of the decay of the autumn, the new possibilities for botanical study presented by the season, then I would survive, and stave off the feelings of anxious horror that had dogged me throughout the summer, through the intensity of my feud with Hume. Today, outside, with rosy cheeks from the fresh morning, I did not give David or my other enemies a single thought: they had no control over me here, they could not touch me where I was, free in my heart. I realised how ridiculous I had been to see their agents everywhere around me, in the vagrants who passed through the woods in search of some food, in the labourers waiting to go to work or resting outside in the early evenings, in other wandering ramblers I had seen on the hills, even in the children of the village who no longer fled at the sight of my clothes, now grown familiar to them. I realised that I was not, in fact, the protagonist of reality, I was not the centre-point and focus of a malicious plot or conspiracy, I had acted strangely, had been carried away, in the grip of a psychological malady worsened by the state of my body. It was as though I were finally restored to myself, for perhaps the first time in years.

But soon the weather turned again, and my mood has changed with it. There were a few warm days afterwards, almost the same temperatures as the best days of summer, with bright skies and warm golden light. These were fine days, on which I walked further through the heathlands and the peaks to the north than I had done before, into increasingly hilly and beautiful countryside, darker and more impressive than that in the immediate vicinity of the house here – enormous moors with the last brightness of the heather still blazing forth. I have had perhaps a week of this feeling of happiness; I took pleasure in everything; I was outside so much that I could ignore the tension in the house easily, and I slept better, not exactly well, but better, physically exhausted and content from my long walks; my work progressed in the evenings, quite easily, at an enjoyable pace, neither the painful grinding nor the desperate fury with which I had been writing before. I was happy to find myself thinking about my childhood, I could see myself back there, I felt as if a straight line had led me from there to here, that things in my life had, in fact, worked out fairly well. In this state of contentment I managed to forget all of my grievances against the world. Then I woke up to an icy morning, the insides of the windowpanes frozen, outside cold and wet and still mostly shrouded in darkness, the weak light of dawn barely breaking into the room. I tried to go out to walk but knew almost immediately that it would be a bad day for it; the winter wind had returned, and I could feel it cut through me as soon as I opened the door – pulling my clothes tightly around myself, I still set out for the sheltered woods, but they were dark, inhospitable, wet and barren. It was as if everything still clinging to life had given up and died overnight; the leaves that had still held onto the branches, gold and red, ready to fall, had curled in on themselves and blackened, staying on the branches shrivelled or lying in hard black piles of mulch; the rich and deep smells of the last few weeks had become more sepulchral, rotten, noxious. It was not yet winter, with the bright hard frost, it was a dark and sad day, and my mood responded to it naturally. After less than a mile, it started to rain; large, cold drops which sliced through the depleted foliage of the woods like knives. I turned back, defeated, and returned to the house with a stony weight in my chest.

It's late. Away from the house I fall into a thicket, tripping over a hole made by an animal. I lie there in the damp foliage. I cannot see in front of me. Leaves rustle somewhere overhead. My eyes close and I doze for a while. The night creeps around me – they might be looking for me now, or they might not be – why would they? For a moment it is as though I have broken free at last, I realise that nobody at this moment has any interest in me, as long as I simply lie here in this thicket in the pitch black of night, far from home, alone. If my body could acclimatise itself to these conditions I could stay here forever, fading into the undergrowth. No need to move or eat or drink, I could remain here, leave my body here and let my mind and soul drift off to wherever they need to be, abandon my physical form, letting it rot, off I go, happy and drifting free above the clouds, no more aches, no more pains, no more memories, no more sensations, no more, no more, no more, no more.

There needs to be light to illuminate a self, something needs to shine on it. Some selves are transparent and allow the light through. Others are opaque and reflect the light, bouncing it off them. I seek transparent selves, and try to make my own ego so. The flatterers and false friends have opaque selves, merely returning the light that shines on them. How does a person make himself transparent, open to the light of examination shone by others? How do I reveal myself openly in all of my qualities and characteristics, the true and honest representation of my personality? Is such a thing even possible? Does it not depend on the intention of the person to whom I am trying to show myself? All I can do is provide a fragmentary account of the history of my feelings and my behaviour, one which is necessarily incomplete, and it is up to them to reconstruct some larger, complete whole from those disparate pieces. I cannot ensure they do so accurately, and the risk of misinterpretation, the tendentious and wilful denigration of myself, is something which troubles me. So I must try to be as full as I can in my account, and in writing it I must omit as little as possible, so that I may stand the best possible chance of being properly understood in a fair and considerate manner by some reader in the future. Perhaps that reader is not alive yet – but I hope that one day my account of my sins may be found by someone who is able to read it correctly, to understand it immediately, to feel as though a light has been shone on them, one passing through a perfect piece of glass, losing none of its pure qualities, unobstructed by smears or stains. I do not want to be a mirror and tell my readers about themselves; I want my work to be a transparent sheet of glass that allows them to see who I was, that allows them to judge me on my own terms, without interference.

When I think back on my earliest efforts, those errors which brought me into contact with the friends who would go on to ruin my life, I laugh, almost, at the warning to myself that I ignored. A man who will be all his life a bad versifier, or a third-rate geometrician, might have nevertheless made an excellent clothier. This may be the truest sentence I have written. If only I had taken my own word at face value, if I hadn't even written it down, if I'd remained in the obscurity I enjoyed in my home country, during my apprentice-ship, fixing watches, the precision of the craft, the long, slow hours measured out by the deafening syn-chronisation of the room full of timepieces of various sizes. Yes, that was it, that was my opportunity to be happy, content with a trade, working with my hands and eyes, steady, regular, obscure.

Out into the woods, out of the wind, the light barely penetrating the canopy, there is a thick coating of moss on the ground, soft, damp, the smell of decay, dead leaves, mould. A large clump of mushrooms growing out of the cracks of one of the new walls – the same wall I watched being built in the spring. A buz-zard circles above a field, perhaps a kite. The dark close soil. Raindrops on the leaves. Wood smoke, peat smoke. Brown, churned up empty fields, lying empty. Out on a walk, I struggled to shift my near-permanent mood of despondency. The over-active past few months which required my constant vigilance, and the writing of an enormous number of letters defending myself to seemingly everyone under the sun, have left me exhausted and depressed. The anger and right-eousness I felt in July have given way to a gloom which hovers about my head like flies around a corpse. I cannot now find much pleasure in the changing state of the woods and the shifting colours of the landscape, even a bright and clear-skied day, with warm sunshine and a light breeze, even companionship with the people here who I am sure care about me seriously and genuinely, cannot lift me out of this stupor. Usually I am able to walk off the anguish, to distract myself, but I feel depleted and incapable of joy or contentment. I start to wish again that I were dead, that I might be taken in the night. I walk along lanes, the leaves so thick underfoot that they completely bury the tracks I follow, and instead of being able to give thanks for living to see a rare day of beauty here, I feel the tears come to my eyes and a heavy sense of loss overcomes me. I am acutely aware of having erred at some point in my past, having followed unthinkingly a path which was wrong, and only now realising how far from my true place in the world I have strayed. Not just one mistake but an unending chain of errors, missteps, naivety, obstinacy, cowardice, weakness and all the rest of my moral failings confront me wherever I turn. The countryside here suggests to me all that I have lost and can never hope to regain, all that I abandoned, all that was taken from me before I had a chance to enjoy it fully, but of which a shadow still remains, indelibly on my heart, reminding me of the absence, of the poverty of my life now, the complete lack of hope or optimism, the knowledge that all that is left open to me is a gradual worsening, a slow deterioration, of not just my body, not just my mind, but of everything I have held dear, everything I have cherished, all of it will fade and decay, and I can only hope that I am gone before all that I have loved is truly eroded.

There is a difficulty in treading the same ground over and over again, in the opposition which arises in my mind between absolute significance and total irrelevance. Nothing new arises, I revisit the same spots, the same moments, the same encounters, none of which ever reveal a fresh element or perspective, I cannot seem to unearth any new detail or develop any new interpretation of the events of the past. They confront me as dead weight. And so I become confused, unsure whether I have imbued the events of the past with a significance they do not in fact have, or whether I am in fact missing some key to their secret meaning. Have my experiences been significant or have they not? I am bored with them, stuck on them, I find myself trapped by the same predicaments again and again. Because these things happened to me, I cannot release myself from the grasp of their memory. But do they have any real meaning or bearing on my life? Were those looks of which I was the recipient real, did they mean anything in themselves, or have I manufactured some meaning and then allocated impressions from elsewhere to events that were in fact completely unrelated? Does any of this matter – and to whom? This is a major difficulty which is worsened by my loneliness. I must be the sole judge of these things. Only I hold the power of signification, having no one to say to me: That doesn't matter, don't worry about it, no, you're misreading things. What I want is to be soothed and then chastised: caressed and kissed by a friend who, once I've recovered myself, will firmly tell me to pull myself together. Instead I have to trust my own flawed judgments of events and people; but how can I trust my evaluative faculties when they have misled me so often? Nothing happens here and so I am forced to invent. Solitude and idleness are the causes of these mental phantoms, these unsolvable conundrums, cul-de-sacs of thought. Am I doing this to myself, or is it some kind of malign spirit? I feel only a deep chasm of confusion, an inability to grasp any fixed certainty. My thoughts are erratic, stopping, starting, repeating, never clear, no conclusions reached, no propositions advanced, just the imprecise feeling of trying to relate a physical feeling to the mental event which accompanies it. How much of this rambling is caused by my physical illness? If my body worked as it would in full health, would I be thinking like this, or would my mind be free to occupy itself otherwise, with something less painful, less maddening, less boring, less pointless? If I could go a day without pain, perhaps I could also go a day without experiencing these mental contortions.

The old lie of the first person: the untruth which claims it is possible to reproduce an account of happenings in the distant past as if they had happened to the same body suggested by the word I as the I now writing. All that has gone; it's over and it can't come back, and good riddance to it, it happened to someone else and it didn't leave an impression which can then be exhumed, dusted off, reconstructed. The darkness descends. Stars and planets emit or reflect light in the sky. The wind whistles through the gaps in the walls. All of this was put here by chance, a series of accidents which coalesced, gained a momentum which could not be halted. It's the same with a life, each day new and the last gone, nothing left of what happened but still the expenditure of the future in the present by the reconstruction of the past. The forces which exist beyond a body's limits, and are exerted on it from without, are in tension with the forces that are constrained and curtailed by the body's limits and which seek the dissolution of this container through their expression. The systole, diastole, the knife through the tissue, calcification and obstruction of a necessary passage, straining, burning, squeezing, exertion, containment, matter expressing its impulses, contortions – on it goes.

The rewriting of a life seemingly becomes an unending task, not just because of the amount of things that need to be included – what I did, where I was, with whom, for how long, how it made me feel, and on, and on – but because of all the things I did not do, thought of but failed to realise, wanted but was too afraid or cowardly to take possession of, all of the desire unfulfilled, the wants unmet, the needs unsatisfied, the plans abandoned – for books, compositions, letters, journeys, relationships, loves – which make up as much of the story of a life as the actual events which did in fact happen. What would a version of my life look like without the fantasies, without the unlived hours spent dreaming, building castles in the sky, the music of the future? It would be less than half a life, more an annal than a history, of no interest to anyone, more like a police report than a biography.

Nothing happens. Nothing happens. The days pass, gradually the pile of papers grows, I live almost entirely in my own head, talking to myself as I wander about, at a loss, unable to account for how I spend my time, with what it is that I occupy myself, I have nothing to show for the last however many months, I am wasting time, but there is nothing I want to do, nothing to distract me, no activity I wish to pursue, I am stuck with myself. On the rare occasions I speak to other people, I quickly lapse into silence, unable to talk about whatever I am expected to, I feel I have nothing to offer in conversations, my contributions are wrong, inaccurate, misguided, inappropriate, crazed. I hold lengthy discourses in my own mind, interrogating myself, attacking myself for my past behaviours, criticising the person I once took myself to be, chastising myself, then changing tack, beginning to praise myself to myself, to exalt myself, I sing my accomplishments back to myself. I relate everything back to myself. I have no other point of reference, no other comparisons, I am the empty centre around which all else orbits, I can't help it, can't unthink myself from these habits, long-held, familiar, easy, comfortable, why should I bother trying to give them up now, why would I try to better myself according to the standards of a world which scorns me and which I scorn in turn? There is no need, nothing to be gained from it now, no chance of reform, of my resignation, no chance of me taking up a false position in the wrongness of the world. All that I have is myself, and that is all I've ever had: the circularity of thought, the obsessiveness, the abnegation and adulation of my own self, turn and turn about, that's all there is, all that's available to me, perhaps all that's available to anyone.

Moonlight lies on the hills like snow. At my desk I work, writing now about my years of wandering, trying to make a career for myself as a musician, or at least a teacher of music. I had many pupils, all in all, though never many all at once. Remarkable how I managed to teach them anything, when at the time I knew nearly nothing – very little indeed. I wandered between towns: Lausanne for a while, Nyon, Fribourg, Berne, never staying long at any of them, often just passing through. Perhaps I am getting mixed up – I visited all of these towns in my youth but I can never remember clearly the order in which I visited them, or the reasons for my going there. What motivated my travels? Sometimes I tried to establish myself in the town, sometimes I was on some errand or other. The years of my life with Maman were full of separations and reunions, drifting apart and back together. Working over these years in my seclusion here, trying to organise a faded series of disordered recollections and impressions into some accurate coherence, I am struck by the ready plenitude of good people I came across in my youth, who I found with ease and regularity. Now it seems I have to search like Diogenes with his lantern, while in my early twenties I was surrounded by people who expressed natural feelings without strain, who were open and honest; I am forced now to associate with the so-called higher classes, who only show feeling as a way of masking an expression of vanity or self-interest. It is as though the people that populated my youth have since become extinct, the race of honest men has died out since the days in which I travelled the Vaud as a singing master who could not read a tune, when I went by the name Vaussore, boasting of my non-existent talent and ability in fits of reckless extravagance.

After a few hours of uneasy dreams, I woke to a mild and grey day, a steady gentle rain on the windows, outside the trees looking miserable. When it rains like this the whole country feels huddled and shrunken, as though there could be no activity taking place anywhere in the world, the atmosphere too inhospitable. Not an extreme of weather, but a general unwelcoming prospect. This kind of day was beginning to feel increasingly normal. I would remain in the house, walking through my rooms again, distractedly taking up my book or some pages I had written the day before, not reading them, my mind on other things as usual, the morning would drift past, at lunch I would swallow something unpleasant in Thérèse's company, and she would either be silent and morose or would quickly run through the old list of complaints again and I would listen in silence. After lunch I would think about going out, stand at the window observing any movements in the clouds, which were a solid bank of unchanging grey, and then decide that I was probably better off inside. I might write, only a few sentences, which would seem wrong the moment I set them down on the page, confused and imprecise, and then I would abandon this activity quickly and with disgust. And so on. It is one thing to live an unproductive life of idleness when you are young and reside in a climate which is conducive to long hours spent outside; it is quite another to do so when you are aged and infirm and the country outside is dreary and wet, inaccessible and forbidding. So many of my days pass in this manner, this enforced lassitude. It is as if I am waiting for something to happen. I don't hear much from anyone at the moment. Sometimes Granville will arrive, but his movements around the country have seemed increasingly erratic of late, to my eyes at least, and I haven't heard from him for some time now. Mary has of course gone with him. Perhaps I should have tried harder with the others who wished to make my acquaintance when I first arrived here. I had wanted nothing to do with anyone, arriving in the condition I did, but now I would relish an hour's conversation with a new face. I still get some letters, but not many. It is as though the great stress and intensity of the summer has burnt through my life, and now I am only left with the embers strewn about me, the discarded remnants; I have achieved the isolation I always said I craved, and I regret it immensely, since it seems that I am destined now to simply wait around here, in this damp province, until I am lucky enough to die. And how long will that take? I feel unwell, but no worse than usual, just the same old familiar ailments. No crisis of the body, no crisis of the mind, just this perpetual gloom, and the gradual fading of the weak day into night.

*

DAVENPORT HAS left again for Cheshire, taking his grandchildren with him. Granville has been away for some time, to take some sort of cure – he may return soon, but I have no word from him. So we are back to our isolation and our lonelinesses, Thérèse, Sultan and I. Thérèse is unhappy and would like for us to leave. She no longer trusts the kitchen servants to prepare our meals, if ever she did, but she is reluctant to cook herself, seeing it as a loss of the position she believes she has gained. So she stands there bitterly among her enemies, hawk-eyed, checking that we are not being poisoned. I think I am safe from them, but less sure that she is. I told Davenport about the conflict between them, and he promised to speak to the servants and remind them of their duties of hospitality. But hospitality is the wrong word, since we are not guests here but tenants: I pay for the use of the house. Anyway, Thérèse goes to buy the ingredients for the meals herself and guards them jealously. It is an impossible situation which I am trying my best to ignore. She longs for Paris, where her mother is ill, though there has been no news for a long time. Of course, I can't go back to Paris, and I can't do without Thérèse, so she must stay with me, despite Mrs Cowper in the kitchen. Meanwhile, my relationship with Davenport's steward here, Mr Walton, is excellent. We still can't speak to each other much, but we communicate largely through affectionate smiles and nods. Occasionally I allow myself to pat him on the shoulder or to clasp his hand. He sees to things, I believe, though exactly what the things are that he sees to escapes me. But he is Davenport's intermediary when Davenport is away, as is typically the case. When he is here, Granville helps by communicating my wishes to Walton, when I have wishes which need communicating to him, but there is rarely that need. I have been feeling recently as if the cloud has lifted again, and my anxieties from the start of the summer have abated somewhat. Davenport's presence has been a palliative; Granville's company kept me distracted, and it has done me good to disburden myself. Nothing from or about Hume for some months now, so whether he is biding his time or has abandoned his plot remains to be seen. I feel a rejuvenation, as though I have gathered the strength I will certainly need through the coming winter. I still grimace at the thought of the frozen landscapes and snow which greeted our arrival here.

Anyone else in my position would begin to hate mankind, but I cannot do so. I have, of course, become averse to socialising, but it is from being hurt too many times in the past. This does not lead me to sustained anger with those that hurt me; instead I feel a deep pity for them, a heart-rending melancholy, that it is so difficult to bridge the painful gap between ourselves and others, that we want to be close to others, but when we come too close we can seem only to hurt them, a hurt no worse than the hurt caused by loneliness and isolation, by withdrawal from the world. I begin to think that I am alone on this earth, that my contemporaries have no feelings of their own, that they are mechanical beings that act only according to impulse, I am the only one who feels truly, everyone else behaves according to codified and pre-established laws of motion. Since I am surrounded by automata, I can begin to calculate in advance what they would seek to do to me; I can unravel their plans by studious attention to what they have already done, which informs me of what they might do next. But no sooner has this idea taken root in my mind than I start to doubt it again; I realise that actually the plot against me is universal, complete and irrevocable, and that it is certain I will end my days in this awful exile, without ever quite working out the mystery behind it. I cannot decide whether the nature of the scheme was crystalline in its predictability or murky and opaque, unclear and shrouded in the darkest enigma. The experience of persecution baffles me, but it also works to elevate my soul. My love of truth started as a mere system, applied ideas, chosen because it sounded virtuous and seemed good. But my adherence to this system has cost me so much that I pursue the truth now with the zeal of a convert; it is my dominant passion, which determines every movement of my mind and body.

I feel as though even the weather here is part of the complex of scheming against me; by keeping me house-bound and agitated, by stopping me from finding the only respite open to me, that of the natural world, I become increasingly erratic, less secure and comfortable in my mind, less capable of defending myself. The weather conspires with my enemies to rob me of my capabilities and my reason. I am weaker by the day, less clear in my thinking. The end must come soon.

The feeling of having taken a wrong turn somewhere, far back in time, down a road which seemed only right, or even natural, at that moment, but which now, clearly, has led you into a dark and unhappy situation, into the isolation and loneliness of this melancholy land, far from any true kindness or genuine friendship; the thought that if only things had somehow been different, then, if you could only have made more of an effort in that place, at that time, with that person, or if you only hadn't said that one thing, or that other, then perhaps, in spite of it all, you might still have a chance of happiness. Perhaps my chance for happiness was missed in very first years, there in Geneva, my only hope for a life of pleasure and quiet enjoyment, simple tasks, craft, my days ordered and secure, my tools laid out, the watches to repair, the familiar faces of the village, the trees, the lanes, the sunsets, no word of the world beyond the next village over, nothing else, rough wine at night, a meal, simple, simple, simple and staid. But no, that was not meant for me, or I was not meant for it. That life passed me by before I had even an inkling that it was there at all. Before I had a chance to make a decision one way or another, the door had closed without my knowing. And that has always been the way with me: before I knew there was a choice to be made, the path had already been taken. But who took the path, if not me?

The familiar restless agitation. Housebound again, I wander from room to room, pick up a book, leaf through a few pages, put it down, stare into space, get up again, walk to another room, pick up some object absent-mindedly, wander into another room, put it down without paying attention, stop, turn around, drift back to where I started, sit with my head in my hands by the fire, my mind blank, toiling, a fragment of a melody repeating itself, trying to think, hoping to bestir myself, the heels of my hands pressing into my eyes, up again, I sigh, I pick up the same book as before, read even less, just a phrase, I close the book, eyes closed again, all day long the same rigmarole. When will the weather change again? I long for a clear, crisp, bright sky, frost on the ground, the earth solid and peaceful, a hard transparent light. Instead, every day sees a thick black wall of cloud obscuring everything, biting and painful winds, a restlessness outside, violent, miserable. It snows in the night, and during the day the countryside is grey with it. I can't keep my mind on anything for long. Usually it is empty on the surface, but I can tell that in the depths there is a constant churning away, a bubbling anxiety, fermenting, which sooner or later will spill over and shift me back again from this restless melancholy into some worse state of mind. If only I could find some peaceful distraction, but I am too miserable to take pleasure in anything now. Some childish activity would be enough, but I am forced to act as if I were an adult, I cannot play games, I am forced to work over my troubles and the sources of my pain again and again.

Now that we are alone again, no more visits, little correspondence, few opportunities to get out across the hills because of the weather, books all sold, spinet out of order, what am I supposed to do with myself? I have always tried to find isolation, a quiet retreat from the world, have always wanted to be alone and idle, but idleness loses its appeal when it is enforced. The only activity that seems to be open to me now is to write, and so I do that with the greatest imaginable reluctance. Going over it all, all the old nonsense, my miseries and pleasures; it all seems hollow; the joys are gone, the happiness flown, I can't get them back now, and thinking them through again and again just dispirits me. The inanity of my routine here depresses me: all day the same things, Thérèse's complaints, the servants' surliness, my work still there on the desk, gradually accumulating, seemingly of its own accord, but a source only of tedium and loathing for me. I am not even able to sleep what remains of my life away, since as soon as I lie down and close my eyes it is as if I see David's face looming before me, the look of malignancy and blandness combined – I open my eyes and he's gone; I worry that my mind is beginning to fracture under the pressure of the boredom I see stretching out in front of me. I need distraction, but I find none in this house. What shape does a life have? At some point it takes on a set of dimensions, proportions, a size, but these are always at risk of change, variance, they are unstable. It's only at the point when a life is interrupted, through death, that its final shape can be determined, but even then it remains unclear. It requires careful and difficult work to sketch out the shape of a life, its contours, because life exists as duration, not extension – you can try to recreate it, but it will never be complete; in trying to recount a life, especially one's own, in its true shape, by revisiting all the events, feelings, desires, failings, and so on, of the past, you reshape the life already, you alter it: the time spent going back over it all is time that could have been spent otherwise engaged, better occupied. All the waste and mistakes of a life have to be included, even if they're better forgotten, they need to be recovered somehow, wrenched back out of oblivion to take their place among the other ephemera and junk. While life is lived it is potential: a series of half-finished tasks, intentions, processes begun and abandoned, uncertainty, false starts, dogged misguided continuations; both out of our control and entirely our own responsibility. In death those open-ended potentials harden into something else, they calcify and become fixed, bulky, unwieldy, they come to be representative of the life even if they were recognised as erroneous even while they were still nascent. How can I form my life to the shape I want it to be? By leaving a set of dimensions, as complete as possible, guidelines in written form, so that it will be clear what exactly the content and form of my life was in fact.

The ringing in my ears is back, and with it the loss of balance; combined with the increasingly severe weakening of my vision, I begin to worry that soon I will be no more than a blind and deaf head, forced to remain in bed all day, with only the various pains in the parts of my body I can no longer see to remind me that I'm still alive, despite everything. My digestion has been bad recently too: the food here is abominable, but even if it were nectar from Heaven I would still retch it up. My body wants nothing to enter it, but when something manages to make its way in and stay in, then my body wants nothing to leave it either: yesterday one of the largest stones I have ever passed, a jagged rock out of my urethra, combined with agonising constipation. Probably I face the prospect of another infection now, which will mean a week sweating out the piss that I can't pass through more conventional means.

Across the fields to Calwick, through the snow, the hedgerows barren. It took longer than usual and was hard going; the lanes channel the wind, which cuts through me. Nothing stirred, it was as if the world had frozen completely, I didn't even see a single bird – for two slow miles each way – not even crows out in the fields. A low pink sun seemed ready to extinguish itself at any moment. Granville has returned to the area again; he is in bed, unwell. It seems that everyone is unwell. He has arthritis, which is much worsened by the low temperature, and gout – which everyone here has, except, somehow, me. I am used to being the invalid, and it gave me some slight pleasure to visit a sickbed, to sit by Granville's bedside and speak to him in a solicitous and caring tone for once, rather than the usual reverse scenario. But I will certainly pay for my visit: the cold wind on the walk back made my temples feel as though they had been squeezed, my ears rang, my kidneys felt a deep, dull ache. How people can bear it here in the winter is beyond me; those that can afford to do so will leave – Granville will be away again as soon as he is capable of travelling – but so many remain behind out of necessity, with nothing. The winters in the mountains are difficult, certainly, but the people there expect the snow and ice, they anticipate it and prepare accordingly. Here is comes on always as if for the first time, and people end up freezing to death beneath the hedges.

Where is my brother? What happened to him after he left Geneva? We never saw or heard from him again. Dead now, probably. His absence a wound which I sometimes worry will never close. But what could he have done for me? His absence has been no worse than that of my mother, dead from giving birth to me, or my father, who left Geneva out of pride and abandoned me to some master – I have been alone, without

family, for so long now. I have made my family elsewhere. Maman; Thérèse, who I still sometimes call
aunt. There have been some who I thought might have
been my brothers: but I was too effusive with them,
too expressive. David. Again and again I am forced back
into my own self, trapped in my isolation, orphaned
and alone.

In bed, sick, for the past few days; the world shrinks to
the corners of the room, the pains in my body, the
ringing in my ears, I hurt, I try to sleep but fail to get
more than a few minutes rest at a time, neither am I
ever quite fully awake. My mind wanders – a kind of
manic distraction possesses me, everything I have
been dwelling on or thinking about recently becomes
jumbled and confused – my days in a sickbed at
Maman's; her feeding me soup; the time I wanted to
eat the morsel she was chewing, so I told her I had
seen a hair on it, and then sucked up her half-chewed
food when she spat it out – I confuse Thérèse for
Maman when she attends to my catheter. The fluid
seeps from out of me. I sometimes imagine it is David
tending to me, his unwieldy and indelicate paws
roughly inserting the rod into me – or I imagine him
sitting in a corner of the room glaring at me, I feel that
I must not look at him directly, though I know he's
there, but it seems too that someone is standing over
my bed behind me, I am curled up and on one side, I
have to hide myself from their gaze, which spears and
penetrates me, pins me to the mattress – I feel beset

by enemies again, in bed the smallest details of each recollection become magnified immensely, each minor detail, imagined or remembered, becomes astronomical in size, pivotal in importance, I dwell obsessively on words I have spoken, words I have heard others say, on tones of voice, on glances, glares, winks, nods, looks, smiles, frowns, the raising of an eyebrow, the not raising of an eyebrow, I run it all around in my mind compulsively, I can't stop thinking – and yet, at the same time, a part of my mind seems to detach itself from this cyclone of examination, seems to stand above it, criticising it, recognising the absurdity of it, how wrong my ideas have become, how unreasonable my suspicions are, how they are motivated by the condition of my body and the mood I am in, the deep and childish self-pity. This part of my mind, superior, cold, starts to lecture the lower churning part: Stop it, it says, stop thinking about that, leave that alone, put that down, just rest now; but the admonishments are unheard, unheeded, and the constantly working depths of my mind continue their permutations. The compulsive part of my mind has always managed to be more concerted in its activity, more reliable, than the part of my mind which tries to stand above itself, which pretends to reason and calmness, acting as if it were the sensible voice of the normal world, which promotes logic and quiet, linear progressions of proof and certainty, while the lower portion leaps across events, ignores juxtapositions of time and space in reality and connects everything that has happened to me with everything outside of my own experience, seemingly at random but ultimately in the service of some much larger schema: the fact, indisputable now, of my persecution and mistreatment at the hands of a gang of conspirators. It is in bed, when I am unwell, that nothing obstructs this process of induction, no external reality can break in to distract me from scratching away at the irritations of my unhappiness. When I am outside I can think my empty thoughts, I manage to occupy my mind, but here I am stuck in a state of bodily inertia, which is compensated for by this mental hyperactivity, which gives me no rest but pursues me even into the few rare and brief glimpses of the dreams I retain upon waking.

I sit before the fire, trying to ease the pains in my stomach. Sultan's head rests on my leg, my hand rests on Sultan's head, my eyes are half-closed, in front of me the amber glow of the fire expands to fill my field of vision. I begin to drift away. In another armchair Thérèse sits, knitting. The rhythm of her needles clicking is the only sound in the room. I doze. I am interrupted. Thérèse begins to speak, but it is not a beginning in any real sense, it is a continuation of an old and familiar theme, a fugue, rotating through its permutations. I let it wash over me, gradually feeling the sharpness of her words burrowing into my mind: No, it is too much, I have put up with too much, for so long, and now my poor mother is dead, buried in some pauper's grave probably, my poor old mother, in a hole in

Paris, and we can't even go to visit her, it's too much, we can't go to see her final resting place, we can't set foot there because of you, your behaviour, your writings, my home is closed to me because of you, my life is ruined because of you, you, who treat me as if I were a servant, have treated me as such for so long, as if I was hired help, that's it, a nurse, a maid, there's no love between us now, no, no real love, not like there was once, not for some years, no love like there once was between us for some years now, no, no, we are separated completely, I have to treat you like a child, tend to you, how pathetic you are, disgusting, I give you the catheter, put it in, take it out, clean it, disinfect it, that's the closest we get to intimacy, no pleasure for either of us there, me jamming the rod into you, you groaning in pain, my hand around you, flaccid, the blood, the infections, reeking, I hate it, it disgusts me, I won't do it any more, it is nauseating, I'm here with you with nothing to show for my life, no pleasures, no joys, there's nothing for me now, nothing at all for me, everything has been wasted in your company, our children abandoned, all of them, because of your pride, here we are, oh yes, with nothing, nothing but misery for both of us, stuck in the middle of nowhere, the arsehole of the world, nobody can understand me, the servants disobey me, despise me, they treat me as if I were worse than shit on the rug, worse than your ugly dog, your so-called friends refuse to sit at the same table as me, won't acknowledge me, how do you think it feels for me, I am alone, worse than alone because the only person for me to talk to here is you, who I loathe, and I'm condemned to tend to your needs, your sensitivity, your whims, while I'm looked down upon, spat upon by visitors, you call me your aunt, gouvernante, you lie, these lies, fables, stories, you make them up so nobody knows the truth about our relationship, nobody will suspect you, but they all know, they see through you, they know who you are, they think I'm vulgar, they think I'm stupid, but I'm not, I have done the honest work of a Christian woman and I have behaved better than any of your friends, who betray you, humiliate you, the same friends who lured you here, to this shithole, you fell into their trap, they want to keep you locked away here, to humiliate you even further still, good for them, good, let them ruin you, but leave me out of it, let me go back, there's no warrant out for me, you can't do without me but I can do without you, I only stay because I loved you once, once, you were kind to me once, you loved me once, maybe somewhere I love you still, or could do again, but I can't disentangle my life from yours because you have ruined me, taken the best from me, you employ me, you're no husband to me, you hope you'll charm some rich twenty-year-old into loving you instead of being stuck with me forever, I don't know exactly what you think you'll be getting up to with her, I know exactly about your condition, I know how it pains you to get even the first stirrings of an erection, you're an old man, soft and sore, pathetic, oh yes, I wash the sheets after you dribble your piss out onto them, I wash the rods, I deal with the stench, the blood, your whimpering, your bad moods, I nurse you, I baby you, and as soon as you are able to get out of bed and go outside you start chasing after a child, it's disgusting, why are we still here, why don't we leave, take me home, take me back, I hate it here, I hate the people, the weather, the country, the villagers, the house, I hate it, I hate all of it, my life is a misery, I have nothing to live for, it's your fault, it's your fault, I hate you, why can't we leave, it's because David has you where he wants you, David has you, yes, he's out-smarted you, that's for certain, you're a fool, you're an idiot, you think you know so much but you don't know anything, you idiot, you're goose shit, wet, bland, why don't we leave here, the cook wants to kill me, the food is poisoned, we'll die here, let's leave, I want to go, I hate it, the cook is putting ashes in the food, cinders, she spits in it, she'll kill us both, we have to leave ... and on, and on, the poison in my ears, the same com-plaints, night after night, every evening, I doze and Thérèse continues her dirge, mourning her life, mourning her position, and I can say nothing in response to her, because I know she's right, she's right, everything she says is true, and I relish it, the humiliation she makes me suffer, the aspersions she casts on me, yes, I lap them up, yes, I need her to tell me exactly how I have wronged her, why she feels the contempt she does; this, day after day, is my evening entertainment.

It is the past that makes the present bearable, especially to someone for whom the future holds no promise, no appeal. Whenever possible I spend my days immersed in the old joys, long gone now, but all the more precious to me for the knowledge that I once experienced, the knowledge that I once had the capacity for pleasure. How much longer can I keep this going, when my state of mind depends so much on external conditions? If I cannot distract myself I will become unwell, but I am already unwell: my body betrays me, it creates the conditions which encourage my unease to ferment and spill over. At the moment I feel that I only have occasional flashes of lucidity, which tear across the dark morass in which I spend the majority of my waking hours, and I see my situation for what it really is, more mundane, less urgent than I had deluded myself into thinking. I recognise myself as delusional in these moments, but these flashes are brief, they don't last long; soon they fade and I slip easily back into the comfortable familiarity of my suspicion. Thérèse jabbed the catheter in today: no tenderness from her at the moment. The pain has been bad recently; the weather, the same complaint, already familiar. I daydream about the last time I urinated with any satisfaction, a lengthy, forceful, crystalline stream – ah! – not at all like the few pathetic drops I have been forced to squeeze out with great concentration every half hour or so for the past week. With my head on the pillow I hear my pulse throbbing in my ear. I kept hoping the sound would stop so that I might be able to go to sleep. I look at my hand, without colour against the sheets, illuminated in the very faint light which seemed to remain in the room, though I can't tell from where it shines. My eyes adjust to the darkness of the night. With them open, I lie on my side, staring at my hand, listening to the blood circulate in my skull, and I am without thoughts, I simply look without seeing and listen without hearing. Nothing seems to exist outside of the bed, there is no world beyond the sheets, past the limits of the mattress. I am still, alert but not fully conscious, in an interstice between sleep and waking, narcotic. I have no sense of how long I have been lying here. After a while – which may just have been a minute, or many hours – I begin to feel a pressure in my legs and my upper back, a restlessness, and I involuntarily change my position to assuage it. As soon as I have moved it is like a door has opened, and everything I had not been thinking about rushes in: the state of insecurity in which I am forced to live my life, my position here in a foreign country, the enemies I have made, Thérèse's unhappiness, the failings of my life, the abandonment of my children, my isolation, my loneliness, all of it in a chaotic admixture in my mind, each element jostling for its due attention, pointing fingers at me, demanding that I acknowledge and repent of each sin I had committed, each failing for which I was responsible. I get out of bed after feeling the unrest in my mind reach a pitch of desperate urgency and walk to the window. Outside, the night is black, the sky opaque. The pane is cold and my breath condenses on it. I rest my head on the glass for a minute, in some half-formed hope that this might stop the process of recrimination that was cycling through my brain – but of course it does nothing. Eventually I light a candle and sit down to write, taking myself back once again to Annecy, obsessively, to the very first days after I settled with Maman, after Turin, when I managed to ingratiate myself into her household, the first steps along what I thought at the time was the path towards my truly deserved happiness, in among the neatness and order of her house and gardens, the comfortable sweet calmness of those early days, when I was overjoyed, when everything delighted me, when everything seemed assured, as if I had found my place on earth after my years of wandering, I thought that I would soon be dead and that there was no possibility of me being cast out from Maman's house, how wrong I was, how many years I have lived through since then, how much more I have done since that time, since I felt that spurious sense of security which I have longed for ever since, which I lost when I chose to seek some kind of acclaim in the eyes of the public, rather than being content with where I was, that small and contained Eden.

I sat there on the ground, on a slope above a lane in the countryside. How old was I then? I sat on a verge above the lane. I sat on the verge above the lane with my mind on Hell. Would I go to Hell, or would I be saved? I was just a boy. No, older than a boy. A young man. No longer a boy. Older than I should have been. Older than to play games with the idea of eternal damnation. I sat on the verge above the lane. I reclined on the grass, the sun on my face. A warm day in late summer. I thought of the torments which certainly would await me after I died. I thrilled myself with my imagination. I started working myself up into a state of great excitement thinking about it, but just before the culmination of this ferment I felt a cooling, as if a cloud had passed across the sun. I was eighteen. I had been lying on the grass verge above the lane, absentmindedly throwing stones at a tree across the way. Of course, I am short-sighted, and I was then. I couldn't see the tree. What was it? An elm? A beech maybe? I couldn't see the tree then and I can't remember it now. I was eighteen. Nothing else was on my mind: just Hell, and whether or not I would be going there. Sunshine. Birdsong. I felt the stones in my hand, small muddy pebbles. Clods of earth. Cold and damp soil. A quiet and bucolic scene. My mind in Hell. I sat there for hours. Perhaps it was only one hour. Perhaps only a quarter of an hour. I sat there, thinking of Hell and throwing stones at the tree opposite me, never once hitting the tree. A beech, an elm, an oak, a fir, a pine? A yew? Not a yew. A sycamore? I don't remember. I can see myself sitting there, clear as day, but I can't see the tree. I had not hit the tree with a single stone. Of course not: I am short-sighted, and I was then. I sat there thinking of Hell, the crescendo of self-titillation giving way to gloom and despair, my face growing longer and longer, my stomach shrinking in on itself, beginning to feel nauseous, afraid even, yes, I was scaring myself, thinking about Hell and whether or not I could end up there; me, who had never done anything wrong, nothing in earnest, everything I had done was done in innocence, I was as free from sin as you could hope for. I was eighteen at the time, a young man, no future in front of me, nothing to count on, no prospects, free, happy, I suppose, in my way. I thought about my misdeeds. My crimes. My mistakes. Nothing serious. Masturbation. Nothing serious. My desires. Nothing illicit. Nothing bad enough to merit Hell. No, nothing too bad. But I carried on throwing stones at the tree opposite me, and I didn't hit the tree once, and I started to feel increasingly certain that I was wrong, that my misdeeds and my crimes could in fact amount to sins, that I might actually end up in Hell after my death, and that I could not hope for anything else, for anything better. I throw the stones and I became absolutely, unshakeably sure that I would be going to Hell, yes, straight there, and soon, sooner than I would like, if I didn't begin to mend my ways immediately. I started on this descent into myself, self-recrimination, shame, pain, pain, my heart thudding inside me, I sat up on the verge, still throwing the stones at the tree opposite me. Suddenly something inside me recoiled, as if it had reached a limit. Well, what of my sins? I was young, I was only eighteen, after all. Eighteen! Who hadn't done what I had done at this age? My sins, surely, my so-called sins were not cardinal, they were at worst venial, I could do penance; perhaps I didn't even need to do penance, it didn't matter really. What did they amount to? I was young. I prayed. I believed in the mercy of God. Eternal bliss awaited me. And as soon as I thought that word, bliss, I recoiled again, the same descent as before; no, not bliss, there would be no bliss for me, no grace of God, it was closed off to me, especially to me, and down I went, my mind running on, cataloguing my errors, my sins, my misdeeds, my lechery, and I slipped into the gloomy certainty, once again, that I would, no doubt about it, end up in the fires of Hell. And this oscillation carried on and on, back and forth. The same heights, the same lows. I don't know how long I sat there. I didn't have a watch. All the time I was there, my arm mechanically threw stones at the tree, I don't know how there came to be such an accumulation of stones on this verge, but there seemed to be plenty, they came easily to hand, perhaps they were left there for the very purpose I was putting them to, left by the benevolent deity. The oscillation between gloom and hope carried on for some time, and eventually I decided that I'd had enough. I decided that I had to resolve the problem, to cut the knot. Thinking about it couldn't resolve it, thought is infinite and useless in questions like this. So I bargained with the tree, with the pebble in my hand, with God, with the saints, with the whole universe around me, I struck a deal: if the next stone I threw, after having thrown so many already, if the next stone I threw hit the tree opposite me, I would not be going to Hell.

I didn't ask for Heaven. Note that. No guarantee of bliss, just a promise that I wouldn't go to Hell. Limbo or Purgatory would be fine. I had not hit the tree once, in the whole time I had been there, throwing stones at it. It was not a bargain in my favour. If I hit the tree, just once, with this next stone, then I wouldn't go to Hell. And I threw the stone, I didn't wait, I threw it, it hit the tree, a resounding thunk, a bird disturbed, the silent lane echoed, perhaps I am exaggerating, it hit the tree, anyway, it hit the tree and I knew I wouldn't go to Hell. I wondered if I should wait for a sign of my new covenant, the appearance of the Virgin, perhaps, or even a minor saint, interceding on my behalf, but I decided better of it, and I leapt to my feet and started off on my way along the lane, and never again set my mind in Hell, considering that I had wrapped up that question quite nicely indeed. Yes! But now, of course, I think that it was a poor bargain I struck with God. Yes, a poor bargain. I don't know if I can believe the youthful exuberance I felt in my certainty of eventual redemption, and I have been so many times in Hell during my life on this earth, so frequently at the worst and lowest ebb, subject to the most vicious torments of my alleged and former friends, of the whole stinking world around me, that I think in fact that I struck a bad deal with God, that I might instead have preferred to have my experience of Hell postponed until after my death, that this life has been punishment enough for me, and that whatever could have lain in store for me before the stone hit that tree must surely have been a manageable ordeal compared with what I have had to endure since.

Our second winter here is thick around us. The lanes are impassable once more, with enormous snowdrifts. Even Granville cannot make it the short distance from Calwick. In a few weeks he is going south again for some sort of cure, and then I will be decisively alone once more. Davenport is still in Cheshire, and I have no idea when he might return; certainly not until after Christmas at the earliest. He has his illnesses too, which are also intensified by the weather, but he is wealthy enough to go somewhere with more clement conditions when necessary. Boothby is always off somewhere, often in France; he doesn't write because of the arthritis in his hands. Everyone is ill. I still receive some letters from friends abroad, but not so many. My one true friend – so I thought – Lord Keith has long since stopped writing to me, begging that he is too ill to continue an extended correspondence. I had dreamt of moving to his estate in Scotland, even more removed from the world, seeing out our last hours together among the thistles and the pines. But Hume is a countryman of Lord Keith, and no doubt has somehow worked to poison his mind against me. I loved him dearly, Lord Keith, even calling him my father. This is what hurts me so much: David has not been content merely to degrade my reputation only in the eyes of the public, about which I do not care in the least. No; he must go further still and alienate my friends from me, stretching out his malignant claws to tear the trust and love once felt towards me from the hearts of those I held dear. I have lost friends before, countless times, but each time it happens through no fault of my own it hurts with a degree of pain I had previously thought unimaginable. The wind howls down the chimneys and still I try to get on with the work. Thérèse's conflict with the servants has begun again, and reached a higher pitch: I would rather be with all the devils in Hell than alone with them for much longer. The worst of them is a ninety-year-old woman, a former nurse of Davenport's, who he feels tenderly towards and inevitably will not hear a word spoken against. She sits in the kitchen all day, by the fire, snug in her corner, pretending to peel vegetables – if her ailments allow it – and talking, in her impenetrable dialect, to the cook. Since Thérèse is also at a loss regarding how to spend her time, she finds diversion in arguing with these two; it's a toxic combination of malice and boredom which motivates them all. The tensions and mental disturbances I experienced earlier in the summer are starting to worry me again. I don't know if I can survive another crippling bout of the anxieties I felt then; I have heard little news of David recently, though I'm sure he has been busy – why would the plot be paused, when they have me exactly where they want me to be? But it seems that I can go nowhere else for the time being, and I must suffer another English winter – I have never known such biting cold, though I'm sure worse conditions are yet to come.

*

WE ARE NOT welcome in this house any more. I have written to Davenport to see whether he knows what has been happening under his roof, what is being done daily to Thérèse and me, since Christmas at the very least, but I have not heard back from him. He ignores me, or the post is somehow delayed – but I suspect the former. Why won't he come; why doesn't he write? Perhaps he is ill. But I am ill too, and the conditions in which I am forced to subsist day by day are making my complaints increasingly worse. My head rings constantly, ranging from the tremulous buzzing in my ears to the crescendo of a steely drone. This is not helped by the behaviour of Davenport's old nurse who, even though she is only an old woman, slight and frail, stalks around the house, slamming doors, kicking over logs, rattling crockery, a constant noise emanates from whatever region of the house she is in. She mutters under her breath constantly; I don't understand her but Thérèse claims to, and as soon as an insult is perceived, Thérèse starts haranguing the old woman, in a mixture of broken English and slang from the gutters of Paris. I had forgotten she knew such language, but I suppose the state of desperation she is in has brought it all back. The nurse inevitably raises her own voice in rejoinder, and then hobbles off to the kitchen to air her grievance to the cook, who also despises Thérèse and who I'm sure is beginning to poison us in earnest. I am forced, of course, to take Thérèse's side, but I would prefer to keep as far out of it as possible, as Mr Walton does, who looks on these scenes with bent brow and rheumy eyes, sometimes offering me a pained smile of solidarity which is sharply rebuked by his colleagues. The situation is not tenable. We must leave unless Davenport comes to resolve things soon. The people here are not part of the general plot against me, of that I am relatively sure, though Thérèse doubts it and frequently suggests to me that they are in league with my other enemies. But that is a step too far, even for me. They are malevolent out of boredom and isolation; their remoteness from the intrigues of the world and their lack of education should, I would have thought, make them simple, open, honest, but through a life of servitude I suppose they have been exposed to the hypocrisies of the upper classes and it has inevitably corrupted them. The same thing happened to me in my own youth, but I fought against the poisoning of my soul and struggled to retain a true sense of who I was in spite of the people I was forced into association with. In this place they have resigned themselves to their degradation, and seek only to retain their positions in the household, which they seem to think are threatened or disturbed by the presence of Thérèse and I here.

We have now been here for a year, as of today. The situation with the servants is intolerable – it must soon reach a conclusion. Davenport said he would come fairly soon, but I have had no news from him – delays, delays. He has not yet visited this year. I begin to suspect him. I have written again, insisting that he appear by a certain date – within three weeks – and if he doesn't then I will be confirmed in my suspicions. I know he still corresponds with David, even though before my arrival in this country they did not know each other – Davenport claims they have had no intercourse whatsoever, but I don't believe him. I feel constantly agitated; my body is falling apart and it feels as if there are hot embers inside my skull. It has rained or snowed every day for about five months – or at least it seems to have done so – my nose drips relentlessly. I begin to think that I am not in England at all, but again in some antechamber to Hell, waiting for the beginning of some even worse torment. It might be time to leave – but where to go, with whom to stay? Cerjat may still be an option – I will offer to live with him if Davenport does not show himself by the end of the month. Cerjat and I have not met, but in another recent letter du Peyrou insists that he would be sympathetic and trustworthy, and with him I would be with a compatriot, a fellow exile, free from the monitoring and surveillance of my enemies; for a while at least. Out in the woods today I came across a glow of lilac sheeting the ground, the bluebells emerging, the first crocuses of the year peeking out along a verge. Finally, some colour after the past months of grey and black weather, the harshness of the winter here. It is late for them, according to the books, and I expected more of them, but they are still beautiful and they cheer me up slightly. Walking back along the stream, I saw a heron standing erect and still in the water, eyes rotating in its skull but otherwise looking as if it were the last sign of winter, the last frozen object waiting to unthaw.

I have been forced into a corner. I can see no possible movement in any direction. My life and situation feel disordered and unrecoverable; I am beginning now to be conscious of just how unsustainable things are as they stand. How much longer will this reprieve last, and what am I going to do when it's over? I will have to go backwards, since there is no route forwards left to me – but where is backwards? Everywhere behind me is gone for good; return would be impossible. We can never go back to where we were, but must keep inching our way forward, in blindness, in the hope that the path ahead will not be too difficult, too unstable, too impassable. It is as if on either side of me there is a ravine, and the thin plank which supports me above the abyss is rotten through.

Mrs Cowper put ashes and embers in the food. She served the soup in bowls strewn with grey dust, a lump of coal still glowing in the middle of the dish. Thérèse looked as if she would murder the woman. I could not speak, I was shocked, apoplectic. At first I could not understand what was happening and I raised my spoon as if to begin the meal. I don't know what action of mine or Thérèse's pushed Mrs Cowper over the edge, but this retaliation was a step too far, and a sign that things had finally reached their conclusion. We left the house under a cloud. On the desk in one of the studies I left a note for Davenport informing him of our decision; most of our possessions were left behind; I placed the keys in the locks of our trunks so it would appear to the servants that we would be returning soon. Then I waited outside the house, pacing back and forth in a state of complete agitation and confusion while Thérèse went to the village to find someone to transport us away: we agreed to pretend that we would not go far at first. In the coach we travelled towards the east along the back roads. I didn't want us to be discovered or followed by my enemies; we travelled for days through some of the most dreary and depressing landscapes I have ever had the misfortune to see – flat, with infinite fields of beet and cabbage, an enormous grey sky, impossibly large, unbearable to look at, all of the countryside unremittingly monotonous and dreary, imposing and claustrophobic in its complete blandness. I wanted to reach the coast and leave the country, but I didn't want to go through a major port; I thought perhaps we could stow away, or obtain a passage on a fishing boat that would drop us ashore in the dead of night, away from customs inspectors and officials, away from police and guards. We would leave under cover of darkness, we wouldn't be heard or seen; but I had not thought how far the sea was from our residence, which is in almost the exact centre of the country; I just told the driver to head east – I had Cerjat in mind still, he who had nothing to do with the good David, or with my other enemies, I thought we could stay with him for a few days while we

got our bearings, perhaps I could entrust the manuscript and some papers to him, perhaps I could borrow
money for a passage, something like that. I took off my
Armenian gown, I wanted to appear inconspicuously,
so I was forced to resume the wearing of breeches and
the discomfort that comes with it. It was one of the first
days of our second spring in this country. The complaint in my bladder had fortunately been less severe in
the past few weeks, but I had still been having trouble
sleeping; endless nights in which I saw the whole scope
of the plot in which I found myself entrapped, the whole
scheme, to what uses David had been put against me,
the disappointments I had received from my treatment
by Davenport, all of it revealed to me in crystalline
detail and at length. I picked away at it again, the old
familiar wounds. In the coach my bladder started to
hurt again, I suppose from the tension and mental
strain of the situation. We travelled onwards and eventually, after what seemed like days of these unending
fields, we arrived at a small town. I don't know how long
it had taken, my mind was in a stupor. The driver said
he would take us no further: he had already gone too
far. He and Thérèse quarrelled over money. What was
the name of the town? Spalding. Were we close to the
sea? We were not. Still some days away. Our journey
had passed in something of a fugue and I had lost my
grasp of what day it was. What were we doing? How far
could we be pursued? The invisible net around Wootton could extend even here. The landscape around
Spalding depressed me immeasurably. I did not quite

know where to find my unmet countryman. I wrote to everyone I could think of: Davenport, General Conway, Cerjat. Davenport wrote back immediately, and proclaimed that he was horrified to hear where we had gone to, dismayed at the behaviour of his servants, apologetic, giving excuses for his delay in coming to us, for his silences, for the mistreatment we had suffered in his house. I wavered slightly in my opprobrium and considered returning to him, but eventually I decided against it: he offered excuses, not reasons, he would not quite admit his fault, he would lure me back into the same false position that we were in before; I could not go back to Wootton, certainly not as long as those servants remained in the house. To Conway I wrote, begging his protection – as the Lord Chancellor he must be made aware of what is happening under his jurisdiction. I realised that he was linked to David, who he employs, but I assumed that so important an officer of the state would be trustworthy and would have had no part in David's schemes or conspiracy. I promised Conway that I would never breathe a word abroad of the ill treatment I had suffered on this island if he would provide me with a guard to Dover, someone to escort me onto a boat returning to terra firma. Some locals overheard my struggles to communicate and involved themselves in my affairs. They had been gathered in the corner of the inn, drinking wine and ostentatiously reading some pamphlets. One acted as an intermediary. I gave my name and they all looked at me in surprise – yes, even in this backwater they had heard of me. The individual who had taken it upon himself to act as my interpreter addressed a remark to me in Latin. I did not catch its meaning. Pompous gesture. I replied in my own language. They introduced themselves as a book group, another of those self-described learned societies which seem to emerge like mushrooms in every small town in this country with more than half a wealthy man. Even here I could not avoid the catastrophes of education. We spent a few days at Spalding, trying to evaluate our situation. After a few days I received a rather laconic and dismissive reply from Conway, almost insulting, in which he said he was unaware of any danger I might be facing, he knew of no threat to my life, and that any ordinary postillion should suffice to get me to my destination. Davenport wrote again, bidding me return to Wootton. I thought about it – perhaps I had been rash in my leaving; he was prepared to forgive my behaviour; I had mistreated him. I felt a ray of light break through the storm clouds which had been lingering in my skull. Yes, perhaps, perhaps we should return to the rabbit warrens and the mosses – Granville and Boothby, who both seemed to earnestly cherish me, for once – perhaps we could still be happy among the moors of that dark country. But no, Thérèse was unhappy there and would be unhappy to return. Since her mother's death she had continued to gnaw at me to return to France, and I could not do without her. No; no – the clouds gathered up again and it was clear that we had to leave – I did not feel secure in this country. I saw spies everywhere and I was too conspicuous. I could not understand or make myself understood. The sky seemed to only exist in various tones of black and light grey. Money was beginning to run low: Davenport still owed me one hundred pounds from the sale of my books and etchings, money which would have done me much good, but I refused to ask him for it: the manner in which we had left his house made it awkward, I still didn't trust him entirely and I had not yet settled my last payment of rent. Of course, this anxiety worsened my condition. Cerjat was a hope: my compatriot might lend me money, or might allow me to stay with him. He came to Spalding to meet me, from some other remote part of the county. He declined my offer of coming to live with him, muttering something about his wife, something about the unpleasant landscape which I would find unappealing, and he was reluctant to take possession of any part of my manuscripts, not wanting to shoulder any responsibility for their contents or the safety of their author. Du Peyrou had suggested him but I found no help from my countryman. I suppose because the word from Geneva had reached even this far-off corner of our diaspora. All seemed to have failed me. I wandered around the town in a blue, ordinary coat, feeling agitated when I was by myself but managing to present an attitude of good spirits when I was in company, either with the priest of the town, with whom I walked a little, or with the learned gentlemen who continued to try to discourse with me. I was forced to dissemble, to assume a calm manner, so as not to attract any unnecessary attention from my enemies or alert my invisible guards to my whereabouts. I had been risky in writing to Davenport and Conway, since they might communicate my whereabouts to David, intentionally or not, or my letters might again be intercepted and read. I had abandoned my cipher out of urgency and a need to be understood. I felt torn between two elements of myself, the true feelings of agitation and fear, my overly active imaginings of agents of my persecutors around every corner, and the jovial and calm public face that I had to present while out on the short and uninspiring walks I took with the priest. I decided to adopt a false name – Renou – and to become increasingly vague about my origin when I spoke to anyone. Part of me chafed at this necessary deception, but I also started to enjoy it, as if it were a game; I was reminded of the time, long ago, that I had passed myself off as an Englishman, Mr Dudding, and the romantic opportunities that had arisen through this falsehood. I longed to cast off my true identity, disrobing myself of the name Rousseau, and slip into the costume of a new individual, obscure, humble, natural, not the target of an international conspiracy. But I knew I was too old now, and too famous. If only I had foreseen all this in my first naïve graspings for public acclaim, then perhaps I might have been less tempted to wander from Maman's side at Les Charmettes, less willing to alienate myself from her love by seeking higher stations in life than those which were my apportioned lot. Perhaps this experience of persecution is simply the punishment I must receive for the crime of hubris; my desire to climb the ladder to fame and public recognition, the ladder which I have now kicked out from underneath me. After the disappointment of my meeting with Cerjat, and the news from Conway that Thérèse and I would not be accompanied by a guard on our journey to Dover, we left Spalding as soon as possible. We had to leave. I was told that there was no passage to the Continent to be had anywhere on the coast near to this part of the country, which anyway was more than a day away in the first place. The best thing, apparently, was to return through Dover, the way I had first come. But perhaps this advice was more misinformation. I didn't know how far the scheme reached, whether now it was government spies that were trying to keep me here. Perhaps in Dover I would face arrest. But I saw no other option and we left. We were at Spalding for a week. I was forced to sell the last remnants of our silverware on the journey, my mind being in such a condition that inevitably I undersold myself and our money quickly ran out. I had kept enough aside to ensure our passage back to the Continent, but other provisions would be difficult to obtain. The pressure of poverty I felt around me worsened my mood considerably – I had been without money before, but this time it seemed that my want would be fatal, that I would soon be in a state of total ruin, which I suppose is what my enemies ultimately wanted. I could brook no further delay: we had to leave England immediately, as soon as we set foot in Dover we should be put on a boat. I could not afford, emotionally or financially, to remain in this country any longer. Even with arrest warrants out in my name in France, I knew I would still be more secure there – there were still people there on whom I could count, du Peyrou would advance me money against the new collection of my works, as distasteful as such a project now appeared to me, perhaps he would pay me in advance for the work I had completed at Wootton – it was good that I had not left anything with Cerjat after all – I could now give it to du Peyrou, with the instructions that it should only be published after my death, and he could be guaranteed that he would not have to wait long for that stipulation to be met. I tried to sleep during the journey, which we made as rapidly as possible, nearly two hundred miles. Of course, I could not rest, and my bladder was the worst it had been for some months. My mind was wracked with anxiety. I felt like a hunted animal trapped in a snare, and for what? What had I done? My friends had betrayed me, but I did not know why. I could feel the rope tighten around me. I had to leave. Thérèse talked incessantly about how she had hated England from the minute she had set foot here, she complained, in an unceasing dirge about everyone – Boswell, who had brought her over and incompetently slept with her, Mrs Cowper, Davenport, David, Boothby, Granville, everyone – everyone, whether or not they had erred or sinned against me, whether they deserved it or not, whether it was justified or not, Thérèse attacked them all, at length. My mind could no longer hold any distinction or opposition, all boundaries started to blur, there was no longer any difference for me between what I understood by the word friend and by the word enemy – all were enemies, or could become enemies, there was no hope for loyalty or truthfulness. Yes, I recognised that I had mistreated my friends, and that in turn they had mistreated me, they had become enemies, but perhaps they considered me to have made them act so. I didn't want any of this. I longed to be back at my father's knee, watching him work, delicate and precise motions, the specialised work, nothing but honest pay and honest prideful labour, no infamy, me reading Plutarch to him, his sad tenderness in his grief for my mother, I wished to be back there, I should never have left, should never have written a single word, I recant it all, I would welcome another burning of my books, another effigy of me strung up, this time I will light the match myself, if only I could hope to be finally left in peace after it all goes up in flames. My life has been a mistake, a single vast mistake in the hopeless search for comfort – that was all I wanted, not even happiness, just comfort! I never asked for happiness, only to be left alone, in peace. We arrived at Dover. The gulls were audible from miles away. I wanted to leave immediately but we were told that passage across the sea would not be possible for some time due to the rough conditions, the strong winds. The strong winds! There was only a mild breeze. I ran down to the sea to see things for myself. It was early May. A spring day. Sunshine. The sea was salt-grey and almost flat. Conditions! What conditions? Too rough! I ran back to where Thérèse was waiting with the boatman and insisted we were taken across immediately. The man refused. Taciturn. The sea was flat. This must be part of the continued plot against me. There was no way for me to escape the machinations of those who wish me harm. I sat and wrote more letters to the people I thought were responsible for my imprisonment on this island, promising that I would never write another word if only I were permitted to leave – I would never publish again, I would never set foot on this rock again, I would keep to myself, I just wanted to leave. A few days, we were told. In a few days. Maybe tomorrow. There would be a sailing when the wind dropped. The wind! It was a whisper. I would welcome this breeze on the boat, cool and refreshing, restorative, certainly not dangerous! The breeze is a gale, they insisted. I insisted it wasn't. The weather was still calm, as far as I could tell, but I was assured repeatedly that we would not be able to cross. I began to understand the meaning hidden behind these words: if I set foot on a boat headed to France I would be arrested and made to remain in this country: they did not want me to spread word of the ignominies I had suffered at their hands here. Again I wrote to Davenport, I wrote to Conway, I promised that if I were allowed passage out of this country I would never publish a word about my experiences. The world would not know about the hypocrisy of this self-professed liberty-loving nation. The boatsman said we could sail as soon as the wind dropped. We rested at the inn. Thérèse was pleased to be able to talk to someone other than me, and left me by myself while she engaged some other travellers in conversation, I don't know what about. I sat, agitated, looking out of the window, my mind racing, as I felt again the net closing around me, I was certain that I would die in this town, waiting for a passage. Bad weather they had said, dangerous crossing, but the air was still and the sky only lightly clouded, the gulls sailed serenely above; I thought of the first crossing eighteen months ago, my first time at sea, thinking that I was leaving my persecution for safety at last, thinking I would be embracing the bosom of freedom, how wrong I was, how naive, how falsely I had been treated since – that last crossing was rough, certainly, the deckhands all vomiting and cursing, David green, remaining below deck, moaning, the black waves crashing onto the ship, the howling wind, horizontal rain, awful, everyone in great discomfort, but I stood outside, drenched to the skin but firm, exuberant, not needing or wanting sleep, but looking imperturbably onwards to the lights on the coast wavering before my eyes, a bad crossing for anyone else, but not for me; if they could cross then, why not today, the sea is flat, calm, the crossing takes no time, it is a continuation of the plot, the onset of the night, the climax of the action, the end draws near. Food was placed in front of me: fish, parsley. I examined the dish, tasted the herb, which was more bitter than I expected. The same family as hemlock. Perhaps this was the culmination of it all: I was to be poisoned here, done away with, they would be rid of me here, they would not brook a man living his life dedicated to the truth. I spat out the herb, I stood up from the table, threw the dish to the floor. Thérèse looks at me in irritation and anger, begins to speak to me, but I don't hear what she says, I leave the inn as quickly as possible, I run down to the sea, I see the boat we are supposed to take, the shoreline is deserted, the boat is out of the water, high and dry, but I clamber in, I scale the side and throw open the cabin door, slamming it behind me, I'm here now in the dark, a chink of light shines through the boards in the ceiling, I hear my breathing and the cry of the gulls outside, I lie down flat on my back and watch the grey light break into the gloom, here I am, this is my place, this is where I will stay. I see my final hour approaching. I am resolved to go and seek it, and to die or else be free; there is no longer any middle way. I hear the waves outside lapping at the shoreline, and as I close my eyes I am transported back into the forests I wandered in my childhood, the sound of the wind high up in the branches above, rustling the leaves, the branches tenderly rubbing against each other; I am back there now, back in the forest, walking, alone, free, happy, happy.

Also available from grand**IOTA**

APROPOS JIMMY INKLING
Brian Marley
978-1-874400-73-8   318pp

WILD METRICS
Ken Edwards
978-1-874400-74-5   244pp

BRONTE WILDE
Fanny Howe
978-1-874400-75-2   158pp

THE GREY AREA
Ken Edwards
978-1-874400-76-9   328pp

PLAY, A NOVEL
Alan Singer
978-1-874400-77-6   268pp

THE SHENANIGANS
Brian Marley
978-1-874400-78-3   220pp

SEEKING AIR
Barbara Guest
978-1-874400-79-0   218pp

JOURNEYS ON A DIME: SELECTED STORIES
Toby Olson
978-1-874400-80-6   300pp

BONE
Philip Terry
978-1-874400-81-3   150pp

GREATER LONDON: A NOVEL
James Russell
978-1-874400-82-2   276pp

THE MAN WHO WOULD NOT BOW & OTHER STORIES
Askold Melnyczuk
978-1-874400-83-7   196pp

HUMAN WISHES / ENEMY COMBATANT
Edmond Caldwell
978-1-874400-85-1   300pp

Production of this book has been made possible with the help of the following individuals and organisations who subscribed in advance:

Julia Aizuss
Joseph Albernaz
Alison's Poetry Commissions
Rees Arnott-Davies
Bethany Aylward
Thomas Beamont
David Bell
Jack Belloli
David Bierling
Charles D Blanton
Paul Bream
Andrew Brewerton
Ian Brinton
Jasper Brinton
Peter Brown
Eleanor Burch
Thomas Bury
Sean Canzone
Daniel Chedgzoy
Alice Christensen
Claire Crowther
Croydon Candles
David Currell
Daniel Daly
Kester Davies
Darragh Deighan-Gregory
Adam Dransfield
John Dunn
Hannah Ehrlinspiel
Andrew Elrod
Andrew Everitt
Allen Fisher/Spanner
Emily Fitzell
Val Fox
Donald Futers
Laura Gill
Jim Goar
Joey Goldman
Giles Goodland
Penny Grossi
Charles Hadfield

John Hall
Andrew Hamilton
LiHe Han
Daniel Hartley
Tom Hastings
Randolph Healy
Simon Horton
Kristoffer Jacobson
Richy & Gill Johnson
Laura Joyce
Christopher Kelly
James Key
Lindy Key
Danny King
Sharon Kivland
Scott Lavery
Monroe Lawrence
Katie Leacock
Johanna Linsley
Frances Madeson
Richard Makin
Michael Mann
Adriana Marshall
Ian Maxton
Tim MacGabhann
Clem McCulloch
Cameron McLachlan
Rod Mengham
Hollie Middleton
China Mieville
Jeremy Millar
Jenny Montgomery
Vijay Nair
Paul Nightingale
Jeremy Noel-Tod
Colm O'Brien
James O'Brien
Toby Olson
Catherine O'Sullivan
Flora Paterson
Sean Pemberton

Hestia Peppe
Willem Pije
Samuel Ramsey
Samuel Regan-Edwards
Will Rene
Asa Roast
Ethan Robinson
Mike Robinson
David Rose
Lou Rowan
Hannah Rowley
James Russell
Steven Seidenberg
Pablo Seoane
Kashif Sharma-Patel
Alan Singer
Valerie Soar
Sean Sokolov
Stryker Spurlock
Andrew Spragg
Joel Stagg
Kyle Stern
Daniel Straw
Alicia Suriel Melchor
Emma Townshend
Tom Veale
visual associations
Alex Rhys Wakefield
Melanie Walsh
Alex Walton
Wash & Dry Productions
Brendan White
Eley Williams
Tom Witcomb
Kate Wood
Patrick Wright
Edward Yates
Clare Young
Bryan Zubalsky
+ 1 anon

www.grandiota.co.uk